The Headless Hound

I glanced around for Drover. At first I saw no sign of him, but then my keen eyes picked up a flash of white on the other side of the thicket. I moved around to get a better look and saw . . . hmmm . . . the hiney and stub tail of a dog sticking up, only the front half of his body was . . . missing.

Holy smokes, had the wild hog taken a slash at little Drover and cut him in half? That certainly appeared to be the case. I rushed over to the spot, expecting to see a ghastly scene, with hair and gore and puddles of blood.

"Drover, don't move, you've been cut in half! Lie still and don't try to talk. Where's your head?"

I heard his faint reply. "I'm not sure. Everything's dark."

"You're losing consciousness. Fight it, Drover, try to stay awake. I've got to find your head. Do you have any idea where it went?"

"I think my head's here with me."

"Oh, good. For a minute there I was afraid it had rolled off somewhere. Don't give up hope, son. Modern medicine performs miracles every day."

"Help! The darkness is closing in!"

"Fight it, Drover, don't give up. Can you give me some hints? If your head is there with you, just tell me where you are."

"Well, let's see. I think I'm in a hole."

HUH?

The Case of
The Missing Bird Dog

John R. Erickson

Illustrations by Gerald L. Holmes

Puffin Books

PUFFIN BOOKS
Published by the Penguin Group
Penguin Putnam Books for Young Readers,
345 Hudson Street, New York, New York 10014, U.S.A.
Penguin Books Ltd,
80 Strand, London WC2R ORL, England
Penguin Books Australia Ltd, Ringwood, Victoria, Australia
Penguin Books Canada Ltd,
10 Alcorn Avenue, Toronto, Ontario, Canada M4V 3B2
Penguin Books (N.Z.) Ltd,
182-190 Wairau Road, Auckland 10, New Zealand

Penguin Books Ltd, Registered Offices:
Harmondsworth, Middlesex, England

Published simultaneously by Viking and Puffin Books,
divisions of Penguin Putnam Books for Young Readers, 2002

3 5 7 9 10 8 6 4 2

ISBN 0-14-230141-8

Hank the Cowdog® is a registered trademark of John R. Erickson.

Printed in the United States of America

For Michael Medved,
a man of courage and wisdom

CONTENTS

CHAPTER ONE

Sleepless Nights

O n the morning of November 1, at precisely nine o'clock in the morning, I noticed that something very strange was occurring on my ranch. It had nothing to do with Plato's sudden disappearance or with an invasion of wild hogs on the ranch. All that stuff came later.

It began with a casual observation. I was in my office, as I recall. I had been up most of the night. No, I had been up most of the *week*. The entire Security Division had been staggering under a workload that would have killed most of your ordinary dogs.

What was the big deal? Well, it was the fall of the year, see, and we had just weaned our calves. Have we discussed weaning time? Maybe not, but

1

maybe we should. It's pretty complicated, so pay attention.

Okay, let's start with basics. This ranch is what we call a "cow-calf operation." That means we run mother cows in our grass pastures. In the springtime, the cows deliver their calves, and throughout the summer the calves live on their mothers' milk. They grow big and strong, the calves do, and then one day in the fall, we round up all the animals in the pastures and separate the calves from the cows.

The calves are old enough to start eating solid food, don't you see, and to get along without momma's milk. And the mommas need some time to rest and put on flesh before winter arrives. This is weaning time. It happens every year and it's part of nature's plan for cows.

So where's the problem? The problem is that . . . well, you just wouldn't believe what happens when we separate the cows and calves. You'd think those mother cows would be happy to get rid of their little parasites—who, by the way, aren't so little. By November, they all weigh four hundred to five hundred pounds. Would you want to furnish groceries for something that weighed five hundred pounds?

Not me, brother. I'd kick him out and tell him

to get a job. But these cows . . . they are *so dumb*! You know what they do when we cut off the calves? They bawl and grieve. For days, they stand outside the corrals and bawl for their five-hundred-pound babies, who stand on the other side of the fence and bawl for their mommies.

It's the worst noise you can imagine. Day and night, honking and moaning, bellering and mooing. Who can sleep through such noise? Not me. Only a rock could sleep—a rock or Drover. Drover seems to be able to sleep through anything, but I can't.

Oh, and did I mention the neurotic behavior of the cows? Once we free them from the drain of having to support their calves, they don't know what to do with themselves, so they pace: from the pens to the water tank, from the water tank back to the pens, from the pens out into the pasture, and then back again. They pace and honk and bawl.

And when they get tired of doing that, they start doing other things that are really weird. They'll chew anything. Why? Ask a cow; I have no idea. They'll chew bones. They'll chew on rocks and sticks. They'll chew the boards on the corral fence. Slim even caught one trying to eat a garden hose. Is that weird?

And you know what else they do? *They chase*

dogs. Honest. No kidding. For the past five days, I had been followed and chased by a hundred and twenty-seven head of unemployed mother cows.

Why do they do this? Again, I have no idea. Sometimes I get the feeling that they . . . well, want to eat me. Don't laugh. Any animal that will eat a garden hose might be crazy enough to eat a dog. But other times I've gotten the impression that they want to . . . I don't know. Adopt me or play dolls with me or something nutty like that.

But the main point here is that at weaning time, I get no sleep. Zero. If I happen to collapse into my gunnysack bed beneath the gas tanks and try to grab a few minutes of moo-filled sleep, one of the old hags will come up and start licking my ears. Yes, they do that, and you know where I stand on the issue of Cow Licking. I won't stand for it, never have.

So what happens is that I'm forced to give sympathy and counseling to the birdbrains. I mean, it's a hard time for them and if I can say a word or two to ease their pain and grief, I'm glad to do it.

Well, I'm not *glad* to do it, but I do it. It's part of my job.

I'll hike over to the weaning pen and have a little chat with the kids—the calves, that is. I'll

4

pace back and forth in front of the fence and give 'em a few comforting words.

"Idiots. Morons. Did you think you'd get a free lunch for the rest of your lives? What do you have to complain about? The hay feeders are full of good bright alfalfa. Go eat. That's what the rest of us have to do. We have to hustle our own grub and chew our own food. Welcome to the real world. Oh, and if you have any problems in the night, just keep them to yourselves. Thanks."

And then I'll turn to the mother cows and give them a little talk. "You cows are SO DUMB! You ought to be out celebrating. At last you're rid of your ungrateful children. They've sucked the life out of you and you're nothing but skinny hags. I'm sorry, but it's true. You're skinny hags, and you know what else? I haven't gotten a decent hour's sleep in five days, all because of you! Pace and bawl, bawl and pace. I'm fed up, do you understand? Go away and leave me alone."

So there you are, a little glimpse at the kind of counseling work we have to do at weaning time.

Where were we? Oh yes, nine o'clock on the morning of November the . . . something. The first day of November, and also the first day of quail season. It was morning and it was nine o'clock and I'd been up all night listening to unemployed cows and I wasn't in the greatest of moods.

And that's when I observed something odd. I was in the office, trying to . . . I don't remember. Reading reports, planning strategy for the week, preparing my precious bodily fluids for another grueling day on Life's Front Lines. It was important, we can be sure of that, and all at once I became aware of a certain . . . odd sound.

Kack-kack-kack-kack.

I lifted my head from the huge pile of reports on my desk and slowly turned my eyes toward the source of the odd sound. I saw . . . Drover. There he was, lounging on his gunnysack bed and gnawing on his foot, if you can believe that.

Kack-kack-kack-kack.

I glared at him for a long moment, hoping he might quit. He didn't. "Drover, could I ask you a personal question?"

His eyes came up. "Oh, hi. Sure, you bet, ask me anything."

"What are you doing?"

"Well, let me think. I was chewing on my foot . . . I guess."

"Ah! Chewing on your foot. I thought that's what you were doing."

"Yep, that's what I was doing."

"Has it ever occurred to you that this foot-chewing creates a sound that is . . . how shall I say this?"

"I don't know."

". . . a sound that is not only disgusting but also very distracting to those of us who have jobs and responsibilities."

He rolled his eyes around. "I never thought of that."

"I see. Would you like to think about it?"

"Oh . . . not really."

"What?"

"I said . . . oh sure. You bet."

I pushed myself up from the desk and began pacing in front of the runt. "Let me be blunt. I haven't slept in weeks and my nerves are on edge."

"I thought you slept last night. I heard you snoring."

"I didn't sleep, Drover. I was tossing and turn-ing and listening to the wailing and screeching of a hundred twenty-seven unbalanced mother cows."

"Yeah, but I heard you snoring."

"I wasn't snoring. I was . . . going over reports. I was working my way through a huge stack of paperwork."

"It sure sounded like snoring to me."

"Sounds can be very deceiving, Drover, and let's not get away from the point of this conversation."

"I already forgot the point."

"You were gnawing your foot—gnawing it and licking it."

"Oh yeah."

"It made a disgusting sound. It bothered me, which brings us to our last question: Why do you chew your foot?"

"Well, let me think here." He wadded up his face and squinted one eye. "I don't know."

"Think harder, son. There must be some reason. If there's not, then you should find something else to do."

"Maybe I was . . . bored."

I halted my pacing and stared at him. "Bored? I'm dying from overwork and the crushing responsibility of running this ranch, and you're *bored*?"

"Maybe that was the wrong answer."

"Yes, or maybe it was the truth. For the moment, for the sake of argument, let's assume that you really were bored."

Kack-kack-kack.

I narrowed my steely eyes. "There you go again. Why do you keep doing that?"

"Well, you said I was bored and all at once I felt . . . bored."

"Ah, there we are. You felt bored, so you began gnawing on your foot. Do you see what this means?"

"Well . . ."

"It means, Drover, that you are chewing your foot out of sheer boredom."

"I'll be derned. I hadn't thought of that."

"Exactly my point. You're doing silly things without thinking. If you're going to do something silly, you should at least give it some thought." I noticed that a pained expression had come over his face. "Now what's wrong?"

"It hurts to think."

"Of course it does. When we don't use our minds, Drover, they get fat and lazy, and any kind of mental work causes terrible pain. But in the long run, it's good for us and . . . why do you still have that tormented expression on your face?"

"Well, I have this urge, this powerful urge, to chew my foot."

"Even after you've thought about it? Even after we've discussed it and brought it out into the open?"

"Yeah, it's getting worse! Help! Oh my paw!"

"Fight back, Drover, resist the urge. There's no reason for it. It makes you look silly, and the sound of it drives me nuts. Remember, it's all in your mind."

"No, it's in my paw, and I just can't . . ."
Kack-kack-kack-kack.

I watched with feelings of great sadness as he

attacked his own foot and began biting it again. Our struggle to overcome his irrational urge had ended in failure, but just then something else occurred that threw this case into an entirely different direction.

You see, we were no longer alone in the office. Someone else had arrived—someone who wasn't welcome.

A Warning
from Pete

Do I dare give out the identity of the stranger who had arrived at the office? Maybe it wouldn't hurt. Okay, it was Pete, our local cat. Mister Lurk in the Iris Patch. Mister Kitty Moocher.

When I saw him lurking there, just outside the office, I whirled around to Drover and whispered, "Shhh! Not another word. We're being watched. I don't want any of this to go outside the Security Division."

"It's only Pete."

"Drover, I'm aware that it's only Pete, and that's the whole point. He doesn't belong to the Security Division and we don't want him listening while we discuss our internal problems."

"Oh, okay. What's our problem?"

I glared into the emptiness of his eyes. "The problem is YOU."

"I'll be derned. That's my problem too."

"Of course it is, and that's my whole point, but we can't talk about it in front of the cat." I shot a glance over at the cat . . . and was astonished to see that he was . . . *chewing his paw*. I dropped my whisp to a voister. My voice to a whisper, I should say. "Do you see what I see? The cat is chewing his paw, Drover, and all at once I'm beginning to wonder . . ."

Kack-kack-kack.

That was Drover. He was chewing his foot again. My probing gaze dashed from Pete to Drover and back to Pete. Do you see what was going on? They were both licking and chewing their respective paws. Even more mysterious was the fact that they were both chewing and licking their *left front* paws.

All at once these two seemingly unrelated actions began to form themselves into a hazy pattern. Something was going on here and I had to get to the bottom of it. I left Drover to his absurd foot-chewing and made my way over to the cat.

Pete wasn't looking at me. He had no idea what was going on around him, and you know what? He

seldom did know what was going on around him, because he was a cat—a smug, arrogant, greedy little creature who happened to be just a little . . . dumb.

I'm sorry, but there's no nicer way of putting it.

Yes, he was just a dumb little ranch cat, and he had no hint that I had just stumbled upon a very odd clooster of clugs . . . cluster of clues, shall we say . . . that seemed to be pulling me into a new and possibly dangerous investigation.

I put on a blank face that revealed nothing, and strolled over to him. "Good morning, Pete. How's the weather?"

His eyes popped open, and he stopped chewing his paw. "Well, Hankie! I didn't realize I was standing right outside your office, and I certainly wasn't listening to what you were saying."

"I know all that, Pete, and we needn't repeat the obvious." It suddenly occurred to me that I had just made a little play on words. "*Pete* and *repeat*. Heh. A little humor there."

The cat blinked his eyes. "I don't get it."

"Fine. Never mind. We don't have time for you to 'get it,' as you call it. I'm a very busy dog." I glanced over both shoulders. "I, uh, noticed that you were chewing your paw just now. Is there some reason for that?"

"Well, Hankie, I'm sure there is, because there's a reason for everything, isn't there?"

Again, I glanced around to be sure we weren't being observed. "Yes. But how did *you* know that?"

"Well, Hankie, I guess it was just a shot in the dark. You know what they say about a blind hog."

"Exactly. A blind hog eats no bacon."

He grinned up at me. "No, no, Hankie. 'Even a blind hog finds an acorn now and then.'"

"Oh yes, that one, but don't try to change the subject, Kitty. I want to know about the paw. I saw you licking it and I want to know why. No more stalling. Out with it."

"My goodness, Hankie, you seem very serious about this. Is something wrong?"

I checked over my shoulders again. "At this point we're not sure, and if we were sure, I couldn't tell you. All I can say is that we're checking out a couple of leads."

"A couple of . . . whats?"

"Leads. Clues. Trends. Things that don't quite add up."

He let out a gasp. "Oh my, so it could be something serious?"

"I'm not at liberty to discuss our work, Pete. Just answer the question and move along. Tell me about the paw."

"The paw. Well, I have two paws in the front and two in the back."

"Yes? Go on. There's more, Pete. I want it all. Why were you chewing your left front paw?"

His eyes widened. "Ohhhhh! So that's it. Hankie, I'm amazed that you noticed."

I gave him a worldly smirk. "See? I knew there

was something here, I knew it. And for your information, Kitty, I notice everything. Now stop trying to wiggle out of my interrogation. Answer the question."

Suddenly his eyes became very . . . hmmm . . . very secretive and cunning, and now he was the one who was glacing over his shoulders. He probably thought I didn't notice, but he was very wrong.

He moved closer and dropped his voice to a whisper. "So you know about the moon?"

"The moon? You mean that it's made of cheese? Of course I know it, Pete. Astrolomy is one of my fields of interest."

"No, I mean the phases of the moon, Hankie. When the moon reaches a certain phase, it causes cats and dogs to . . . chew their paws."

The air hissed out of my lungs. "Pete, that's one of the dumbest things you've ever said."

His left eyebrow rose ever so slightly. Maybe he thought I didn't notice, but I did. I saw it and sent it up to Data Control.

"It's true, Hankie. Did you happen to notice what Drover's doing this very minute?"

"Ha. I notice everything, Pete. Nothing escapes my . . . okay, maybe he's chewing his paw, and of course I noticed it right away, but that doesn't mean . . ." I moved closer to the cat. "What's going on here, Pete? I don't want to fall for another of your sneaky tricks, but I don't want to miss anything either. What's the deal?"

I stared into his . . . hmm, into his moon-shaped eyes, and . . . holy smokes, was that another clue? *Phases of the moon, moon-shaped eyes.*

Something strange was going on here. I had to plunge deeper into the mystery.

Pete took his sweet time in answering. "Well, Hankie, all I know is that the moon sends out powerful signals, and all the animals in the whole world respond by"—he batted his eyes—"chewing their paws."

"Yes, but there's just one hole in your ointment, Pete. Every animal in the world isn't chewing his paw, because I'm not."

"Um-hmm, and if I were you, Hankie, I'd start worrying about that."

I laughed in his face and walked a few steps away. "Ha, ha, ha! Me worry? No chance of that, Kitty, for you see . . ." I paced back to him. "Why should I be worried? I mean, I really don't care what you say, Pete, and there's no chance that I'll believe this ridiculous story, but . . . uh . . . why should I be worried? I mean, just for grins, I'd like to hear this."

"You really don't know?"

"I didn't say that. Of course I know, but I want to find out if you know. And frankly, Pete, I doubt that you do."

His brows rose. "Oh, I do know, Hankie. It would mean that you're *out of phase with the moon.*"

"Out of phase with . . . is that bad?"

A low whistle escaped his lips, and he turned his gaze away from me. "I was sure you knew, Hankie, or I never would have brought it up."

"What are you saying, cat? Out with it."

"Nothing, Hankie. Don't give it another thought. I'm sure it won't happen to you."

"You bet it won't, and do you know why? Because there's nothing to it. It's a pack of lies, just another of your sneaky tricks. Sorry, Kitty, no sale here, and that's all the time I can afford to waste on you today. Good-bye. I have a ranch to run."

As I turned to leave, I heard his parting words. *"Good-bye, Hank."*

On hearing those two words, I knew that I was in serious trouble. Did you get the hidden message? Maybe not, because it was pretty subtitled, so let me explain. Subtle. See, Pete never called me Hank. He always called me *Hankie*, and he always said it in that simpering, whiny voice of his. But this time he'd called me Hank, in a normal voice.

The meaning was clear, and it went through me

like a jolt of electric current. See, the cat knew that I was out of phase with the moon—and even more onimous, he understood the terrible consequences of being out of phase with the moon.

You know what I did? I walked away from him at a casual pace and wandered back to my gunnysack bed. I watched him out of the corner of my periphery and saw that he was drifting back up to the yard. Then and only then did I dare to . . .

You may find this hard to believe, but I began . . . gnawing my, uh, left front paw.

I know, I know. A guy should never take advice from a cat or believe anything a cat says, but on this occasion, I just couldn't afford to take a chance. I mean, this was something entirely new to us. Nobody in the Security Division had heard about these Deadly Moonbeams. We had no idea what kind of catastrophic . . .

There, you see? Another mysterious clue just popped up: CAT-astrophic. Cat. Pete. Do you see the pattern here? No, we couldn't risk a disaster, so I . . . well, I began chewing my paw, and we're talking about serious bites. *Kack-kack-kack.* I was in the midst of this Anti-Moonbeam Procedure when . . .

Drover was there, grinning down at me. "Oh, hi. What you doing?"

"I'm . . . it's very complicated, Drover, and I'm not sure you'd understand."

"I'd say you're chewing your paw, is what I'd say."

I tore myself away from my business long enough to give him a stern glare. "Sit down, son, I've got some news for you."

"Uh-oh. Good or bad?"

"Both. Sit down."

"Can we skip the bad news? I hate bad news."

"Just sit down. We'll take the bad with the good." He sat down. "Drover, the bad news is that the Earth is being bombarded with Deadly Moonbeams." He gave me a vacant stare and said nothing. "Hello? Did you hear what I just said?"

"Yeah, but I can't figure out if that's good or bad."

"It's bad. How could Deadly Moonbeams be good?"

"I'm not sure. I've never seen one."

"Because they're virtually invisible, Drover, and therefore hard to see."

"Maybe that's why I've never seen one."

"That's what I just said. That which is invisible can't be seen."

"I'll be derned. I never would have thought of that. What's the good news?"

"The good news is that we now know why you've been chewing your paw. It has nothing to do with your being a moron."

"Oh good."

"There's a reason for it, a scientific reason."

"Yeah. I'm bored."

"No, it's much more complicated than that. You see . . ." At this point, I launched myself into a full and complete scientific explanation of this mysterious process. Would you care to listen in? I must warn you: it's pretty complicated. If you think you can handle heavy-duty scientific stuff, keep on reading.

CHAPTER THREE

The Deadly Moonbeams

Okay, here we go. I told Drover to sit down and listen carefully.

"First off, you must realize that if you take the *r* out of *moron*, you get the word *moon*. Do you see what this means?"

"Uh . . . no."

"Nor do I, but I'm sure it's an important clue. Now, to counteract the effect of these Deadly Moonbeams, we dogs chew our paws. It's a natural protective reaction, perfectly rational and sane."

"I'll be derned."

"It means that we are now free to chew our paws."

"Gosh, I thought you said it was disgusting."

"That was before we learned about the Deadly Moonbeams."

"I'll be derned. Who thought of that?"

I stared at him for a long time. "Why do you ask? Do you think I would fall for someone else's phony research? Is it possible that you don't trust my judgment in scientific matters of science?"

"Well, I just wondered. It sounds like something Pete might come up with—kind of crazy. But you'd never believe anything Pete said . . . would you?"

I, uh, turned my gaze away from him. "Drover, do you want to go on asking empty questions or do you want to have a good scientific reason for chewing your paw? You can't have it both ways."

"Oh, okay. I'll take Number Two."

"Good. Then chew your paw, and be glad you have a reason for doing it."

He gave me a big grin and began gnawing at his paw. I dropped down on my gunnysack and did the same.

Kack-kack-kack. Kack-kack-kack.

It was kind of a touching moment—two members of the elite Security Forces, chewing our paws and protecting ourselves from the Deadly Moonbeams. It had been a long time since Drover and I had shared such a meaningful occasion. And you know what? It worked. We both survived.

It was a good thing, too, for at that very moment, we heard the sounds of an approaching vehicle. We cocked our respective ears and listened.

"That pickup is coming this way, Drover. Bearing: three-two-zirro-zirro. Range: three hundred yards. Okay, this could be it. You remember that secret report about phases of the moon?"

"Not really."

"Good. This has nothing to do with phases of the moon, so just forget the report."

"I already did."

"This has to do with vehicles sneaking onto our ranch. Do you remember our procedures?"

"Well . . ."

"We'll go straight into Code Three, scramble all aircraft, and intercept him in front of the house, which will put us on a course heading of one-five-zirro. You got that?"

"Oh . . . I'll just run and bark."

I shot him a hot glare. "Don't bark until I give the signal. Do you know why?"

"Well . . ."

"Because, Drover, the success of our mission . . . nay, our very lives, could depend on the element of surprise. We'll maintain Barkosilence until I give the word. Then, we'll go into some Stage One barking and see what happens. Is that clear?" I caught him yawning. "Why are you yawning only moments before a combat mission?"

"Oh, 'cause that's when I needed to yawn . . . I guess. And I didn't think I could wait."

"Ha! You *can* wait and you *will* wait. We'll have no . . ." Hmmm. All at once I felt a powerful urge to . . . uh . . . yawn, you might say. I mean, it was crazy. There we were, poised on the brink of . . . I yawned. "Okay, soldier, go ahead and take a quick yawn. We might need it later on."

He gave me a silly grin. "Well . . . I don't need to now."

"Take a yawn! That's a direct order." At last he took his yawn. "Okay, good. Now we've had a good yawn and our tanks are filled with carbon diego. Stand by to launch all dogs. Three! Two! One! Charge, bonzai!"

Boy, you should have seen us. It was very impressive. Within seconds, we had launched ourselves into the still morning air. We went swooping away from Home Base and roared around the south side of the yard until we reached the Staging Point. There we . . .

HUH?

Yipes, there we suddenly found ourselves on a collision course with . . . it was a pickup, see, a huge ranch pickup, and it was barreling down that little hill in front of the house, and at that very moment—

HONK! HONK!

Okay, it appeared that he was blowing his horn and encouraging us to . . .

"Get out of the road, idiot!"

. . . encouraging us to, well, get out of the road, as you might say. I dived out of the way just in the nickering of time to avoid being smashed. It was a very difficult maneuver, and no ordinary dog could have pulled it off.

Drover came running over to me. "Gosh, that was close. Are you okay?"

In a cloud of caliche dust, I glared after the villain's pickup. "I'm okay, Drover, but that guy's fixing to get a tooth tattoo. Did you see what he did?"

"Oh yeah. He had to swerve to miss you."

"That's not what he did. He swerved and tried to hit me. If I hadn't jumped just in time, he would have creamed me. You know what I think? I think he's a cattle rustler." There was a long moment of silence. I noticed that Drover was staring toward the pickup with dreamy eyes.

Wait. With dreamy eyes, Drover stared at the pickup. The pickup didn't have dreamy eyes. Drover did. With dreamy eyes, he stared at the . . . never mind.

"Hello? Did you hear what I just said?"

"Yeah, but he's not a rustler. Do you see who that is?"

I picked myself out of the weeds, and so forth, and cast a glance to the west. The pickup had pulled up in front of the corrals. Slim stepped out of the saddle shed and waved at the stranger.

"No, I don't recognize the pickup. Who is it?"

"It's Billy, our neighbor down the creek."

"Yes? And is that supposed to be a big deal? Hurry, Drover, we have a very busy day ahead of us."

His eyes were still glazed over. "*She's with him*, riding in the back."

I craned my neck and squinted my eyes at the pickup. I could see nothing unusual. "She? Who is she, Drover? Be specific. We need facts here."

"Oh my gosh, I think it's . . . Beulah!"

HUH?

My goodness, the very mention of her name . . . I studied the pickup with dreamy eyes, and sure enough . . . "Drover, you wait here. I'll go down and check this thing out."

"I want to go too. I saw her first."

"And that's why we need to hold you in reserve. It's a little reward for a job well done."

"Yeah, but . . ."

"Don't argue. I'm doing this for my own good. Now wait here until I give you the signal."

He hung his head. "Oh, drat."

"And we'll have no more of your naughty language. Wait here and chew your paw."

And with that, I left the dunce sitting beside the yard fence whilst I went streaking down to the corrals to greet . . . SIGH . . . the Woman of My Dreams, the world's most gorgeous collie gal, she of the flaxen hair and the long sharp nose, she of the big dreamy eyes, the lovely Miss Beulah the Collie.

WOW!

With my heart pounding in my ears, I went streaking down to the corrals, screeched to a halt beside her pickup, put on my most rakish smile, and looked up into her . . .

Bird dog? Spotted bird dog? Holy smokes, her entire face had been transformed into . . . I mean, where was the flaxen hair, the long collie nose, the . . . HUH?

Okay, relax. You thought Miss Beulah had been transformed into a bird dog? Ha, ha. No, she had merely moved to the other side of the pickup, see, and her place had been taken by . . .

Have we discussed bird dogs? Maybe not. I don't like 'em, never have, and there's one bird dog in the whole world that I dislike even more than the rest. Plato. And there he was, grinning down at me with his big sloppy tongue hanging out of the left side of his mouth.

My rakish look melted, replaced by a curled lip and narrowed eyes. But of course he didn't notice any of it. He was too dumb to know how much I disliked him.

He appeared to be . . . what was he doing up there? Jumping up and down? Running in place?

"By golly, Hank, there you are. Great to see you again, just great. I was just telling Bunny Cakes this very morning, I said, 'Bunny Cakes, it's been a long time since we've seen old Hank.' I did, no kidding. Now isn't that a coincidence?"

"Who is Bunny Cakes? Have you been chasing rabbits again?"

"Oh heavens no! No, Hank, our guidelines are very . . . oh, I see, you were joking, right? Ha, ha. You're the same old Hank, always the life of the party."

"Oh yeah, that's me."

"Right. Great. No, the truth is, Hank," he gave me a secret wink and lowered his voice, "Beulah and I have little names we call each other."

"No kidding."

"I call her Bunny Cakes and she calls me . . . this might sound silly, Hank."

"Oh surely not."

"Thanks. She calls me . . . Honey Bumpers."

I stared into his empty bird dog eyes. "Honey Bumpers?"

"Right. Hey, I know it must sound silly to everyone else, but you know, Hank, we're so happy, we just . . ."

"What are you doing up there?"

"Doing? Oh, you mean the jogging? I've been doing my exercise program, Hank. Quail season's here, and you know what, Hank?"

"No. What?"

"Hank, I'm in the best shape of my whole life. I'm serious. I have a feeling this is going to be the best season ever. By golly, I can hardly wait. How about yourself?"

"Me? Oh, I'm doing all right . . . for a guy with a broken heart."

"Great. Well listen, Hank, I think I'll run some laps while I'm fresh. Maybe you'd like to talk to Beulah, huh? I'll join you in five minutes."

And with that, the creep flew out of the pickup and started running around ranch headquarters like . . . I don't know what. Like a demented bird dog chasing phantom quail, I guess. And he couldn't have looked any sillier if he had tried.

When he was gone, I saw her lovely face come into view above me. My knees began to tremble. Cold chills skated down my backbone, and then hot chills skated back up. My breaths came in short stabbing bursts, my heart began to race, and my head began to swirl. And then . . .

Kack-kack-kack.

CHAPTER FOUR

My Heart Is Dashed to Pieces

It was weird. I mean, when a guy's looking up into the eyes of the most gorgeous collie gal in the whole world, the last thing he wants to do is . . . well, start chewing on his paw, right? But all at once I felt this overpowering urge to . . .

It must have been nerves. Hey, there she was, the same lady dog who had visited my dreams so many times, so many thousands of times, and all at once my mind was whirling like a windmill fan in a storm and my heart was about to jump out of my chest, and so . . . well, it was only natural that I would . . .

She gave me an odd smile. "Hello, Hank. What are you doing?"

Kack-kack-kack.

"Well, I seem to be . . . chewing my foot, I guess you might say. How are you, my little sugarplum?"

"Fine, thank you, but . . . why are you . . . chewing your foot?"

Kack-kack-kack.

"You don't want to know, Beulah. Don't even ask. You seem to be having a good life, so don't bother yourself with my problems."

"Is something wrong?"

I stopped chewing and filled my eyes with the loveliness of her face. "Is something wrong? How can you ask such a question? Isn't it obvious?"

She seemed puzzled. "No, I guess not. Do you have fleas? A skin rash? I don't know, Hank, you'll have to tell me."

I pushed myself up on all fours and walked a few steps away. "All right, Beulah, if you must know . . . I've become a mental and emotional wreck. I chew my foot because I can't eat my heart out. Now do you understand?" She shook her head. "Okay, let's go straight to the point. That bird dog has ruined my life!"

She gasped. "You mean . . . Plato?"

"Yes, Plato. He has ruined my life, broken my heart into eighty-seven pieces, and now he's causing me to chew off my own foot." *Kack-kack-kack.* "There! You see? I can no longer control myself."

"Hank, I just don't undertand what ..."

I whirled around and looked into her eyes. "Beulah, what do you see in that creep? How can you waste your time with a bird dog when you could have ... well, ME, for example?"

She turned away. "Oh, so that's it. I thought we'd talked it out, Hank."

"Talked it out? Ha! You talked it out and I went on living in the rubble of my broken heart, and that's what you see before you today—a broken dog, a dog who's left with nothing to do but ..." *Kack-kack-kack*. "... eat his leg off. That's all I have left, Beulah, and when I chew off this leg, I'll go to the next one and the next one and the next one, and then there'll be nothing left but two ears and a tail."

"Can't we just . . . be friends?"

"Oh sure. When there's nothing left of me but two ears and a tail, we'll be friends, great friends. Maybe I'll go chase birds with your hero. Is that what you want? Would you like me better if I fetched tennis shoes and pointed at stupid twittering birds?"

She sighed. "Hank, I like you just as you are."

"What's to like? I'm a mere shelf of my former self, a husk without grain, a house without a home. Without you, my collie dream, there's nothing here."

"You do get carried away, don't you?"

"Yes, my plum garden, I get carried away, I admit it, and until the day when you . . ."

At that very moment, Billy and Slim came walking up behind me, forcing me to, well, put my mission on hold. That was rotten luck, because I think I had her moving in the right direction.

Billy and Slim were discussing some kind of cowboy stuff.

Billy: "Well, we'll get on down the road. Thanks for letting me use your leather punch. I'll get it back to you tomorrow or the next day."

Slim: "No problem."

Billy: "Oh, by the way, have y'all seen any signs of feral hogs?"

Slim: "What's a feral hog?"

Billy: "Farm hogs that have gone back to the wild. They've had 'em downstate for years, but now they're moving into this area. I was on horseback the other day and rode right into the middle of a mad sow and her litter. It was a learning experience."

Slim: "Yeah? What did you learn?"

Billy: "I learned that you should stay away from 'em. A wild hog is nothing you want to mess with. They're plenty mean, and I've heard they'll tear up a dog. And speaking of dogs . . . Plato! Come on, boy, load up."

A moment later, the Birdly Wonder came blundering in from his romp and dived into the back of the pickup. He was panting, smiling, and covered with weed seeds. I waited for Beulah to give him the bad news—that she had thought long and hard about their relationship and had decided . . . well, to give her heart to ME, you might say.

I held my breath and waited. She gave me a glance . . . *yes, yes, go on and tell the creep*! She gave me a glance and then . . .

I couldn't believe it. The air hissed out of my lungs as the rafters of my dreams came crashing down into the hollow shell of my . . . something.

She didn't tell him to shove off or to get lost. She said, and I mean in a sweet, soft voice, she said, "How was your workout, Honey Bumpers?"

"Great. Terrific. Best one in years, Bunny Cakes. And I guess you and Hank shared a nice talk, huh? Great." He gave me a sloppy-tongue grin and waved his paw. "Great to see you again, Hank. You really ought to get into birds, you know. Bye now, and take care."

As the pickup pulled away, I glared ice picks and bayonets at the jerk, and heard myself mutter, "Take care? One of these days, old buddy, I'll take care of YOU."

Then they were gone, and I was left alone to pick up the pieces of a heart that had not only been broken, but also pulverized. I was in the process of sweeping up the wreckage of my life when Drover came skipping up.

"Oh darn, there she goes and I didn't even have a chance to say hello. I guess you forgot to call me."

I stared at the runt. "What?"

"You said you'd call me and I waited, but you didn't call."

"Oh yes, that. Sorry, Drover, but I was busy with other matters. My life was being destroyed."

"Yeah, she sure is pretty."

"Did you hear what I just said?"

"I love her brown eyes."

I stuck my nose into his face and raised my

voice. "Hello? Will you stop babbling and listen to me?"

"Oh, hi. Did you say something?"

"Yes. I just announced that my life has been destroyed. I'd appreciate it if you could show some concern."

"I'll be derned."

"Is that all you have to say? My whole life, my reason for living, my hopes and dreams . . . they've all turned to mush before my very eyes, Drover."

"Boy, I love mush."

"And all you can say is that *you love mush*? What kind of dog are you?"

"Well, I'm not sure, but huskies love mush."

"Huskies do *not* love mush."

"Well, they talk about it all the time."

"They don't talk about it all the time. For your information, Drover, mush in husky language means 'gitty up.' It means 'pull the sled.'"

"I'll be derned. I thought it meant oatmeal."

"It does not mean oatmeal. If mush meant oatmeal, do you think the huskies would ever pull a sled? No, of course not. They'd go eat, and then who would pull the sleds?"

"I don't know. Reindeer? What does *mush* mean to a reindeer?"

I gave him a withering glare. "Drover, are you

trying to make a mockery of my ruined life? Because if you are, let me remind you . . ."

At that very moment, this loony, meaningless conversation was interrupted by Slim, who had walked over to us. He reached into his shirt pocket and pulled out . . . what was that? A strip of tree bark? A dead mouse? He tore off a bite of it and held it up for me to see.

"Y'all want a bite of my beef jerky?"

My ears shot up. My tail went into Wild Spontaneous Swings and I licked my chops. Beef jerky? Oh yes!

"Well, let's see if you can be mannerly about this. I mean, we ain't slobs around here. Can you sit down like gentlemen?"

Sit like—hey, were we going to share the jerky or not?

"Sit."

Okay, I could sit. I plunked my Hinelary Region down on the ground and assumed the pose of a perfect gentleman dog. So did Drover. There, we waited for our . . .

Slim held the jerky under my nose. My lips began . . . well, smacking, I guess you'd say. Drover's lips were smacking too. I could hear them.

Slim continued waving the jerky under our noses. Our heads moved back and forth with the fragrant morsel. Left, right. Left, right. He got a chuckle out of that, and then he did something really odd. I'm not sure you'll believe this.

You know what he did? After he'd noticed that our heads moved back and forth with the hand that held the fragrant jerky, he started *conducting* us—you know, he held both hands in the air and moved them back and forth as though he were conducting a symphony orchestra. He whistled and hummed a little tune ("Blue Daniel's Waltz," in case you were wondering) and *conducted our heads*.

I thought it was just a little WEIRD.

Hey, I knew what he was doing. He was using our powerful hunger as an . . . I don't know what, but it was an underhanded trick that made us look . . . well, ridiculous. I mean, in my deepest heart, I knew that we looked silly, moving our heads back and forth with the jerky, but somehow I wasn't able to control my . . .

Oh, he made a big deal out of it, standing in front of us and waving his arms back and forth, why you'd have thought he was . . . I don't know, some famous conductor. And did I mention that he provoked us into snapping our jaws in time with the music? It's true, he did.

He even came up with a name for this . . . whatever you may call it . . . this musical experience, I

41

suppose. He called it "Jerky Symphony in Nothing Major." No kidding.

Yes, this was very weird. It was weird that a grown man would do such a thing with his loyal dogs, but it was even weirder *that we dogs went along with it*. I don't know how to explain it, except to say that . . . well, if you wave a piece of jerky in front of a dog's nose, his nose will follow, no matter how badly his heart is broken and how absurd it makes him appear.

Well, old Slim was having the time of his life, conducting his dogs and humming a song, and there's no telling how long it might have gone on if someone hadn't walked up right then—and caught the three of us right in the middle of this silliness.

CHAPTER FIVE

Beulah Returns

It was Loper. The boss. The owner of the ranch on which we were ... uh ... doing these peculiar things.

Slim didn't see him, but I did. I rolled my eyes in Loper's direction, went to Slow Embarrassed Taps in the tail section, and squeezed up a grin that said, "Oh. Loper. I guess you think ... hey, I'll bet this looks a little bit ... we were just ..."

Slim must have sensed that my attention had wandered. His hands froze in the air and he followed my gaze until he saw Loper, who was scowling at us. He pushed his hat down to the bridge of his nose and nodded his head.

"Am I interrupting something?"

Slim's hands dropped to his sides and he began

44

rocking up and down on his toes. "Oh no. Me and the dogs was just . . . funnin'."

"Funnin'. Well listen, Slim, don't worry about all this work we need to get done. What's important is that you and the dogs have a good time out here. I think that's wonderful, a heck of a lot more important than, let's see, welding those feed bunks, hauling in the last cutting of hay, checking those heifers in the Dutcher West pasture . . ."

Slim's face turned red. "You reckon we could just skip over this and go straight to the point?"

A smirk twitched at the corners of Loper's mouth. "The point? Why, what could be more important to the success and survival of a ranching operation than for the hired man to spend quality time with the dogs?"

"Loper, there's times in a feller's life when he'd rather not . . ."

At that moment, my interest in the conversation came to an abrupt end. You know why? Heh heh. Because I had just noticed that Slim's right arm was hanging limp at his side, and his right hand was still holding that strip of jerky.

Heh heh.

I scouted their faces. They weren't watching me, so I, uh, crept forward on silent paws and . . . SNARF . . . suddenly the jerky vanished, shall we say.

I chewed it twice and . . . gulk . . . tried to swallow it, but it was dry and stiff and got hung up in my throat, so I switched my swallowing muscles over to an emergency procedure we call Cram It Down.

Okay, maybe I should have chewed it up a few more times, but after he'd held it under my nose and made me wait so long, hey, I was about to die of Jerky Lust and . . .

HARK!

I, uh, was forced to . . . cough it up, as you might say, before I choked to death. It landed on the ground. I lifted my gaze and noticed that . . . oops . . . all eyes had turned to ME, you might say.

Slim stared at me, then turned back to Loper. "See? Because of you, Hank stole my breakfast."

Loper was forced to laugh. "Some breakfast. Even the dogs won't eat it. Was that some of your homemade jerky?"

"Heck, yeah, and it's good too, the best I've ever made. Dumb dog."

"Well, I guess you could always take it back."

"I think I'll pass on that." He beamed a glare down at me. "Hank, you wasted a piece of my homemade jerky."

Wasted? Ha! Little did he know. *If at first you don't succeed, lap it up again.* That's my motto, and that's just what I did, fellers. I licked it up out of

the dirt, chewed it seventeen times, and rammed it home to the old stomach. It scratched a little bit going down, but I got 'er done.

We call this procedure Jerky Reruns, and it sure works.

Slim and Loper curled their lips and looked away. Slim shook his head. "Hank, have I told you lately that you're disgusting?"

Well, I . . . no, but what did he expect me to do? Leave a perfectly good jerky breakfast and let it go to waste? Forget that.

Loper gave his head a shake and started walking away. "If it's not too much trouble, why don't you saddle a horse and ride through those heifers in the Dutcher West pasture?"

Loper walked up to the machine shed and left us there. A great silence moved over us. I became aware of Slim's harsh glare. "That's what I get for hanging out with a couple of moron dogs. I try to teach y'all couth and culture, and you get me in trouble with the boss." He heaved a sigh. "Well, let's saddle old Snips and check them heifers."

He went into the saddle lot to catch his horse, leaving me alone with Drover. "Why are you staring at me?"

"Well, I didn't get any jerky. I sat here like a

good little dog, and then you gobbled it all down. It wasn't fair, and I'm starving."

"You're not starving, and life is often unfair, Drover. The sooner you learn that, the less you'll eat."

"I had my heart set on that jerky, and now my heart's broken."

"You're heart's not broken. MY heart's broken. Had you forgotten that? I was in the midst of telling you about my broken heart and shattered life, and somehow you got us on the subject of oatmeal."

"No, it was jerky, and you hogged it all."

"It was oatmeal, Drover, or mush, to be more specific. My life has turned to mush, and do you know why?"

"You're a husky?"

"No. Because Beulah loves Plato instead of me. Because she chose a bird dog over a cowdog. That's why my heart is droken, Bover, and you don't even care."

"Yeah, but my name's Drover."

"That's the kind of friend you turned out to be, and I know perfectly well what your name is."

"Yeah, but you called me Bover."

"Sorry. My mistake. I should have called you meathead. Do you know why?"

"Well, let me think here. Because I love jerky?"

"No! Because you've finally succeeded in driving me insane." I marched over to the nearest tree and banged my head against it. BAM! BAM! "There! I feel much better now, and I hope you're happy."

"Well . . ."

"Now, I'm going back to bed. I'm going to sleep and I don't wish to be disturbed. Hold my calls and, most important, don't ever speak to me again. Good-bye."

I whirled away from the little lunatic and started to leave. It was then that I heard him say, "Well, okay, but are you sure that mush really isn't oatmeal?"

I froze in my tracks. For a moment I gave serious thought to going back and wringing his neck. Instead, I hit Full Throttle on all engines and got myself out of the swamp of his mind. I went roaring down to the gas tanks, screeched to a halt, and threw myself into the warm embrace of my gunny-sack bed.

Plato had shot me out of the saddle. Beulah had rejected my love. Drover had turned out to be just as worthless as I had always thought he was. Pete had . . .

Wait a second. Remember that story Pete had told me about the Deadly Moonbeams? All of a sudden it occurred to me that it was all garbage, a typical cat trick, nothing but lies. Yes, I had fallen for it, and Kitty would pay a terrible price for his . . .

I dropped onto my bed, my dear old gunnysack bed, the last friend I had in the world. I had failed in the Department of Love, but I would never fail in the Department of Sleep. Sure enough, sleep came and swept me away from the cruel world.

I had dreams, powerful dreams full of meaning and purpose. I saw myself transported to a better place, a kinder world where there were no cats or bird dogs—just me, all alone with a steak bone as big as a utility pole. It was delicious and I was in the process of gnawing my way through it, when . . .

Huh? The sound of an approaching vehicle? How could that be? Steak bones weren't vehicles and they never drove into our ranch compound. Therefore it followed from simple logic that . . .

I lifted my head and cracked open my eyes. A terrible sight greeted me. Drover. He was sitting on his gunnysack and giving me a silly smile.

"Oh, hi. Guess who's here."

"My steak bone, and don't get any big ideas about sharing it."

"No, I think it's Billy. He's back."

"His belly's on his back? What are you talking about, Drivel?"

"My name's Drover."

"I know your name. I've always known your name. Why do you keep repeating it?"

"'Cause you keep getting it wrong."

I cut my eyes from side to side. "Wait a minute. You're Drover, right?"

"That's what I said."

"Okay, where are we? What day is this? And most important of all, what did you mean when you said your belly is on your back?"

"No, I said it's Billy and he's back. I guess you were asleep."

I blinked my eyes and things began coming into focus. "Okay, I was asleep, Drover, but now I'm back on the job. Now tell me again about your bellyache. How's it feeling now?"

"Oh, pretty good, thanks."

"Good, good. So the crisis has passed?"

"Well, I'm not sure. He just got here and he looks kind of worried about something."

"Ah, so maybe the crisis hasn't passed after all. I was afraid of this." I began pacing, as I often do when my mind is reeling . . . uh, racing. "And tell me again who *he* is, Drover. This could be a crucial piece of information."

"Billy."

I stopped in my tracks. "Billy? I thought you

52

said 'belly.' Well, this throws quite a different light on the case, doesn't it? For you see, Drover, we don't know anyone named . . . wait a minute, hold everything, halt." I marched over to him. "Did you say 'Billy'?"

"Yeah, about five times."

"Just answer the questions, Drover, and let this court decide if you said it five times. Did you say 'Billy,' our neighbor from down the creek?"

"Yep, same guy."

"But he was just here, only moments ago. I saw him myself."

"Yeah, but you slept for two hours."

Suddenly the pieces of the puzzle began falling into a suspicious pattern. I shot a glance over at the pickup that had just pulled into headquarters. "Wait a minute, Drover, do you see what I see? Do you recognize that pickup? Holy smokes, it's Billy, and he's back!"

"I'll be derned."

"And do you see what else I see? In the back of the pickup, Drover. It's . . . it's Beulah! And be still my heart, there's no bird dog with her! She's alone, Drover, she's come back to me!"

And with that, I went flying out to greet my Lady Love.

CHAPTER SIX

Plato Is Missing

WOW!

There she was in the pickup, even more beautiful than I remembered. The very sight of her healed my wounded soul. In a flash, I felt a rush of new life surging through all my bodily parts and fluids, and suddenly I found myself . . . well, jumping up and down. And howling.

A-WHOOOO!

That was odd. I'd never been much of a howler, but that just goes to show what a powerful effect she had on me. One minute a broken invalid, the next . . .

It was then that I noticed Drover. He was jumping up and down, and howling in a childish and disgraceful manner. "Drover, what's wrong with you?"

"Oh my gosh, do you see who's in the back of that pickup?"

"Of course I do. She has finally come to her senses and . . ."

"It's Beulah. She's come to see me, and she's so pretty, it makes my heart jump like a sack of rabbits."

"Drover, please, try to control yourself. You'll give the entire Security Division . . . A-WHOOOO! Holy smokes, I've lost it!"

"A-WHOOO! A-WHOOOO!"

And so it was that, when the pickup pulled up in front of the corrals, Drover and I were . . . well, leaping around in the air and uttering howling sounds, you might say, and we couldn't help ourselves. We had both fallen under the spell of her gorgeousness.

Billy got out of the pickup and stared at us as we . . . uh . . . carried on. "What's got into your dogs? They act like they've taken the fits."

Slim shook his head. "They're both three bales short of a full load of brains, is all I can figger."

There, you see? That's the kind of respect we get from the cowboys in this outfit. Well, for his information, it had nothing to do with so-called brains. It had everything to do with—

A-WHOOOOOO!

I stampeded over the top of the childish, infantile Drover and fought my way to the rear of the pickup. There, I looked up into the adoring blaze in her eyes. Yes, I could see it now. *She loved me!* She had finally come to her senses and had come back to reclaim her Cowdog Hero.

No kidding, I could see it in her eyes, as plain as day, and sure enough, *there was no sign of the bird dog*! At last she had ditched the creep, tossed him aside like the old shoe he really was.

"Beulah, you've come back to me. I knew you would, and you know what? I've been waiting in this very spot since the last time you were here, staring down the road and hoping . . . nay, dreaming that you'd come back to me. And here you are! A-WHOOOO!"

She gave me a . . . well, it seemed kind of a weak smile, to be honest, but then she said, "Hello, Hank."

Did you hear that? Those were the words of a lady dog who had been counting the days and nights and hours, waiting for the moment when she could return to her Beloved Cowdog. But just then, Drover was there, hopping around like a grasshopper and embarrassing all of us with his childish displays.

"Hi, Beulah. Gosh, you're so pretty, all I can think of to say is . . . A-WHOOOOO!"

She said, "Hello, Drover."

The little mutt almost fainted. "Hank, did you hear that? She remembered my name, and you know what? I think she really likes me."

"She's just being polite, Drover. She feels sorry for you because . . . A-WHOOOOO! Sorry, Miss Beulah, but as you can see . . . hey, would you like to hear a poem? I wrote it especially for you. Let's see here . . .

Miss Beulah the collie, I see that by golly
You've come to your senses at last.
I'm feeling more jolly, I sense that your folly
Of loving that bird dog has passed, heh heh."

Pretty awesome poem, huh? I thought so, but when I studied her face, I saw another weak smile. What was the deal? How could she . . . hey, that had been one of my very best poems. Well, I would just have to reload and fire off another one, but before I could get that done, Drover pushed his way to the front and butted into the conversation. "I've got one too, Miss Beulah. Here goes.

Petunias are pretty but so is your nose,
It's more than a functional snout.
It's long and it's graceful and shaped like a rose,
I forget how to make this thing rhyme."

I glared at the runt. "Drover, please. If you can't make a rhyme, get out of the way and stop wasting the lady's time. This is no place for amateur poets."

"Well, I had it just for a second, but then I lost it."

"That's my whole point. Go to your room and think about it. Come back in three weeks." I turned back to the lovely lady and fired off another awesome poem.

"Oh Beulah, I notice your eyes, how they dazzle,
They're showing the symptoms of love.
The pieces are falling in place in the pazzle:
You've given old Plato the shove, hot dog."

Okay, maybe it wasn't my greatest poem, and maybe I was pushing things in trying to make a rhyme out of dazzle and pazzle. But don't forget that this was all done on the spot, under tremendous pressure, and it was a whole lot better than Drover's pitiful effort.

Anyway, I turned my adoring eyes up to her and—HUH? It was then that I noticed a tear sliding down her gorgeous collie nose. I whirled around to Drover.

"Now look what you've done. You've made her cry. I hap you're hopey."

"Yeah but . . ."

"Your poem was so bad, it brought tears to her eyes."

"Well, I was just trying . . ."

"Trying doesn't count, Drover, and when trying brings crying, it's a sign that you're a flop as a poet." I turned back to the Lady in Distress. "Miss Beulah, on behalf of the entire Security Division, I would like to apologize for Drover's ramshackle poetry. He wasn't authorized to deliver a poem at this ceremony, and it's obvious that he needs private tutoring on his rhymes."

"It wasn't Drover."

"Of course it was Drover. I was standing right here and heard the whole thing."

"I thought his poem was cute."

I turned to Drover. "She says that was the worst poem she ever heard." Back to Beulah. "Well, I can assure you, ma'am, that this will be taken care of. We'll send him to his room at once, and I give you my word of honor that he will never . . ."

Her eyes flashed. "It wasn't Drover or his poem. It was *your* poems."

"My poems? You mean . . . oh, I see now. You were so moved by my work that tears sprang to your eyes. Well, I hardly know how to respond, Miss Beulah. I am honored and flattered to the very depths of my . . ."

She shook her head and rolled her eyes up to the sky. "You are so obtuse."

I whirled back to Drover. "Did you hear that?"

"Yeah, but what does it mean?"

"It means . . ." I whirled back to Beulah. "Drover doesn't know the meaning of obtuse, ma'am, so maybe you could, uh, help him out."

She heaved a sigh. "Obtuse means 'you don't understand, or won't.' Talking to you is like talking to a stump."

"A stump? I'm afraid I don't understand. I mean, who'd want to talk to a stump? It would make more sense to talk to the whole tree, although I can't imagine why you'd want to . . . Beulah, is there something here that I've missed?"

"Yes, a lot. Your poems made fun of poor Plato."

"Poor Plato! What's so poor about Plato? He's a professional thief. He's made a career out of stealing girlfriends from worthy dogs, is how poor he is."

Her gaze came down and met mine. "Hank, Plato is missing."

"Right. He's missing, and it's about time you ditched him. A day without Plato is like a day without fleas. I love it. I only wish you'd ditched him sooner."

She shook her head and closed her eyes. "Hank, please listen. I didn't ditch him."

"Huh? You mean . . ."

"Two hours ago he left the house and went out to scout for quail. He was so excited about the opening of bird season.

"Oh yes, birds. He chases birds—when he's not wrecking romances."

Her eyes flashed again. "He doesn't *chase* birds. He finds them with his marvelous nose, and he points them, and he's very good at it."

"Okay, he's good at it."

"He left the house and . . ." She turned away and fought back her tears. ". . . and he didn't come back."

"Hey, terrific."

"We're afraid something terrible has happened to him."

"No kidding? Well, this sort of clears the way for . . . wait a minute. Why are you crying? I mean, at last we're rid of the pest and . . . surely you're not saying . . ." I turned to Drover. He was gazing up at the clouds. "Drover, tell me she's not saying what she's saying."

"What? Oh, hi. Who's not saying what she's saying?"

"Beulah. She just said that Plato is missing. He blundered out into the Real World and managed to get himself lost."

"Gosh, how sad. Maybe we ought to help find him."

I stared into the vacuum of his eyes. "Are you nuts? This is the chance of a lifetime. This is the bad news we've been waiting for. This is . . ."

I couldn't believe my eyes. Drover rushed over to Beulah and said, "I'll help you find him, Miss Beulah!"

The little moron.

CHAPTER SEVEN

The Runt
Has an Attack

Well, this was a bad turn of events. All at once it appeared that Little Drover had somehow managed to seize the inside tractor in the race for Miss Beulah's heart.

She wiped away her tears and gave him a warm smile—the first warm smile she had displayed since she arrived, and the one I had been wanting for myself. "Oh, would you, Drover?"

"Gosh, yes. I'd do almost anything for you."

"I'd be so grateful. I've been worried sick about Plato. Why, if anything happened . . ."

"I'll find him, Miss Beulah. When you're around, I'm not scared of anything. And besides, I'll bet he's not far from the house."

"I'm afraid he is. We looked around the house.

He must have strayed far out into the pasture."

"Far out into the . . ." Now get this. All at once, little Sir Talksalot developed a serious limp in his right front leg. "Oh, darn. This old leg picks the worst times to go out on me, Miss Beulah, and all at once—oh my leg! It's killing me and I just hope . . . boy, I'm not sure how far I can travel on this old leg."

Drover is so predictable. Only moments before, his "old leg" had been good enough for him to be hopping around like a bullfrog and butting into my romantic business, but now, at the first mention of danger and hard work, it suddenly quit on him. What a little faker he was, but of course Miss Beulah fell for it.

"Oh, my. I hope it's nothing serious."

Drover limped and wheezed and groaned. "Don't worry about it, Miss Beulah. I'll ignore the pain. I've got to help you find Plato."

Just then, and you won't believe this, I could hardly believe it and I was standing right there . . . just then the little dunce went down like a rock. BAM! Nose-first into the dirt. He lay there, groaning and twitching and moving his legs through the air.

"Oh, the pain! Drat this leg!"

Beulah uttered a little shriek, leaped out of the pickup, and rushed to his prostrate body. "Drover, what's wrong? Speak to me. Oh dear, what shall we do?" She raised her eyes and looked at me. "Are you going to just stand there? Something's wrong with poor Drover."

"Yes ma'am, something's wrong with him for sure, but the problem isn't his leg. It's his brain."

Her nostrils flared. "How can you say such a hateful thing?"

"Ma'am, I can say it because I know the mutt. He's a permanent harpocardiac."

"Well, at least he offered to help, and that's more than we can say for *you*."

"Hey, Beulah, if you and Drover want to go charging off into the wilderness to look for Mister Quail King, that's your business. If Plato was dumb enough to wander off into the pasture, he deserves whatever he gets."

She gasped. "Don't say that!"

"And besides, what's the big deal? He wandered off into the pasture. He's done that before. He'll find his way back home."

Her chin fell on her chest and she started . . . well, crying. "No, it's different this time. There's danger, real danger. I have a bad feeling about it."

"Beulah, listen to me. There's no danger. It's just a pasture on the ranch. When he gets done, he'll come home."

Her eyes came up, shining with tears. "No, Hank. There's danger out there. Remember what Billy said about the wild hogs? They're on the ranch and we saw them, just minutes ago. If they catch Plato—oh please, Hank, won't you help? I've never asked a favor before, but now . . ." She turned away. "Hank, I'm begging you."

Wild hogs? Gulp.

"Beulah, listen to me. I know you have some strange affection for the creep . . . for Plato, shall we say, but what he did was really dumb."

She gave her head a vigorous shake. "It wasn't dumb. He just . . . he's careless sometimes. He gets carried away."

"Right, and out here in the wilderness, when you make a dumb mistake, you get carried away by wild hogs and coyotes. I'm sorry to put it that way, but that's the truth. And while we're on the subject of bitter truth, here's some more of it. If you think Drover's going to be any help, you're dreaming. He's scared of his own shadow and he couldn't fight his way out of a cereal box."

Drover let out a groan. "He's right, Miss Beulah. It's too dangerous out there, and with this old leg acting up on me, I wouldn't be much help. Oh, the pain! Oh, the guilt!"

Beulah's eyes darted back and forth between

me and Drover. She dried her eyes and stood up. "I see. We came here to ask for help, but I guess we won't get any from you two."

I shrugged. "I guess not. But listen, if old Plato doesn't make it back, I could probably arrange my schedule to, uh, drop in for a little visit, so to speak."

She glared at me and shook her head. "Don't bother. I won't be there. I'll be out searching for Plato, and I won't come back until I find him."

With that, she leaped up into the pickup bed, went to the front, and refused to look at us.

"Beulah, listen to reason. It would be crazy for you—Beulah, are you listening? Stubborn woman. Drover, speak to her. Maybe she'll listen to you."

"Well, I would, but, boy, all at once, this old leg . . . oh, the pain!"

"Drover, you're worthless. At the very time when you could . . . Beulah I'm speaking to you as a friend, and I must tell you that what you're saying is crazy. If you go off looking for Plato, the wild hogs will make hash out of you too, and then where will you be?"

With her back to me, she said, "We'll find out, won't we?"

"Well, I guess we will. Fine. Go looking for the birdbrain and get yourself captured by the wild hogs. Beulah, I never understood what you saw in that guy in the first place. If you ask me . . ."

Just then, Slim and Billy came walking up behind us. Slim said, "Okay, me and my dogs'll prowl through that country north and west of your house. Let's meet at your corrals at three o'clock and we'll see where we are."

Billy nodded. "Sounds good to me. Thanks, bud, I appreciate this. If Loper gives you any trouble, tell him I'll come over and help y'all fix the fence next week."

Slim chuckled. "Oh, don't worry about Loper. He growls a lot, but down deep where it counts, he's really pretty grumpy. A guy has to ignore him sometimes."

Billy waved good-bye and drove away. As they were leaving, Beulah turned around and looked back at us. I waved at her, but she didn't wave back.

Well, that was just too bad. Hey, if she thought I was going to risk my life looking for her stick-tailed bird dog pal, she was exactly wrong. I didn't wish the pest any bad luck, but . . . well, it appeared that he had made his own bad luck, and what was bad luck for him was no bad deal for me. Heh heh. She would get over him.

I turned to my assistant, who was struggling

to his feet. "Well, Drover, she's a beautiful woman, but she's a little short on common sense."

"Yeah, but I feel pretty awful that we didn't help her. I'm liable to feel the guilt all day long."

"But I'm sure you'll find a way to live with it. No, Drover, we made a wise decision. Saving bird dogs is for the birds, and there's no way . . ."

I noticed that Slim was looming over us. "Load up, boys, we've got work to do. Y'all want to ride up front with the executives or in the back where the mutts ride?"

Well, up front, of course. I mean, it was freezing cold . . . okay, it wasn't freezing cold. It was a beautiful fall day, warm and clear, but I sure needed to be up front with the executives. Besides, Slim had loaded his horse into the trailer and hooked it up to the pickup, so there was no view out the back.

Yes, up front.

Slim opened the door and we dogs sprang up into the cab. Actually, I sprang up into the cab, while Drover hopped and scrambled and clawed his way inside. He has short legs, you know, and isn't much of a leaper. But he made it at last, and both of us were sitting proudly on the seat when Slim climbed in and slammed the door. He started the motor and we were off to new and exciting adventures.

We headed east down the county road.

As we bumped along the road, Drover turned to me. "I wonder where we're going."

"We're going to check the heifers, as I recall. Yes, I'm sure that's what our orders said."

"I'll be derned." We rode along in silence, then, "But I thought the heifers were in the Dutcher West pasture."

"That's correct, Drover. The heifers were and are in the Dutcher West pasture. What's your point?"

"Well, we just passed the road into the Dutcher West, so I was wondering . . ."

"Shhhh!" I silenced him with an upraised paw and looked out at the countryside. "Hmmm, something strange is going on here, Drover. We've just passed the road into the Dutcher West pasture."

"Yeah, that's what I—"

"Don't interrupt. If we didn't turn on the Dutcher West road, it means we're not going to that pasture."

"Yeah, that's what I—"

"Will you hush and let me finish? The evidence is beginning to suggest that we're going somewhere else, Drover, but where?"

"Gosh, I never thought of that."

"You need to pay more attention to business. That's one of your problems."

"You don't reckon we're going to look for Plato, do you?"

I gave him a steely glare. "Look for Plato? You think Slim would waste his time looking for a wandering bird dog?"

"Well, I wandered."

"You *wondered*, Drover. You didn't wander."

"Well, I did one time. I wandered out into the pasture, and then I wondered how I would get back home. So I guess you could say that I've done both."

"You've done both, but that's not the point. The point is that wonder and wander are homonyms."

"I ate some hominy once, and you know what? It tastes just like corn."

"That's what it's made of. Hominy is corn."

"Then how come they call it hominy?"

"Because . . . because it comes in a can, Drover. Everybody knows that hominy means 'corn in a can.'"

"I'll be derned. What about corn on a cob?"

"Corn on a cob is not in a can. If it were, it would be called 'hominy on a cob in a can.'"

"Yeah, but what about tuna fish? It comes in a can."

"Exactly my point, and that's all the time we have for questions."

I turned away from the little lunatic and tried

to clear the vapors from my mind. Was this a calculated attempt to drive me insane, or was it merely something that happened whenever he opened his mouth?

I wandered about that, but just then the pickup slowed and Slim made a left turn into . . . hmmm, we had just turned onto a trail that led into Billy's west pasture.

CHAPTER EIGHT

A Rescue Mission

This was odd, very odd.

I turned my eyes on Slim and studied his face for some hint of what the heck we were doing in another man's pasture. Right away, I began amassing clues.

Clue #1: He had a toothpick parked on the right side of his mouth. (Usually he parked his toothpicks on the *left* side of this mouth, so this might have meant something profoundical. Or maybe not).

Clue #2: He squinted his eyes and looked off in the distance.

Clue #3: He slowed the pickup to a crawl.

Clue #4: He rubbed his chin and said, "Now, if I was a bird dog, where would I go?"

HUH?

The pickup was moving again. I turned to Drover and lowered my voice. "Drover, I don't want to alarm you, but we've just gotten word that our orders have changed. It appears that we're now on a mission to find Plato."

"I'll be derned. I thought we decided it was too dangerous, 'cause of all the wild hogs and stuff. Oh, and we don't like Plato."

"You and I reached that decision, Drover, but they've gone over our heads on this one and we may have no choice."

Kack-kack-kack.

"You're chewing your paw again, Drover. Did you see a Deadly Moonbeam?"

"No, I'm scared and I just . . . "

Kack-kack-kack.

"Drover, you're being weird."

"Yeah, but it helps."

"No kidding? Hmmm. To tell you the truth, I'm feeling a little . . ."

Kack-kack-kack. Kack-kack-kack.

Suddenly and all at once, Slim slammed on the brakes, throwing us out of our seats and into the dashboard. We landed in a heap on the floor. What was going on? Had Slim seen something?

I scrambled back onto the seat and met his . . . yipes, angry glare.

"Quit chewing your paws in my pickup. If you've got fleas, chew 'em on your own time."

Well, sure, but the problem went much deeper than . . .

"I can't stand to hear y'all hacking on your paws. Don't you have anything else to eat?"

Once again, he had missed the whole point of the, uh, exercise. I went to Slow Taps in the tail section and tried to explain. See, it was just a simple case of nerves. Jitters. Pre-combat jitters, and then we had the whole problem of the Deadly Moon . . .

He wasn't interested in hearing the truth, and that was fine with me because I wasn't sure I could explain it anyway, so I turned to Drover.

"Well, your weird habits have gotten us in trouble again. How many times have I told you not to chew your paws in public?"

"I thought you said . . ."

"It's noisy, uncouth, and disgusting. How would you like it if Slim chewed his paws all the time?"

"Yeah, but he doesn't have paws."

"That's my whole point, Drover. Slim doesn't have paws, so how would you like it if he chewed something he doesn't have?"

"Well, I guess . . ."

"Don't argue with me. Just say you're sorry and let's get on with our lives."

"You're sorry."

"Thanks. That wasn't so bad, was it?"

"No, I feel better already . . . but I still want to chew my paw."

I looked deeply into the vast emptiness of his eyes, and was about to give him a serious tongue-lashing, when all at once . . . holy smokes, my head was being drawn and pulled down toward my . . . well, toward my left front paw, almost as though some mysterious force had seized it.

I shot a glance at Slim. He wasn't watching.

Kack-kack-kack.

His eyes came at me like balls of fire. "Quit chewing your dadgum paws and get out of my dadgum pickup!"

He stopped the pickup. Well, gee whiz, he didn't need to . . . you know what he did? *He threw us out the door.* Both of us! I was shocked. I mean, if he didn't want us chewing our paws, all he had to do was . . .

Oh well, I didn't care. It had seemed stuffy in his pickup anyway, and did I mention that the cab of his pickup stunk? Stank. Stinked. Stunked. It smelled bad, and I was happy to get out into the fresh air.

After this shocking display of childish behavior, Slim unloaded his horse and tightened the cinch. Then he called us over. I trotted over to him. He buckled on his chaps and hitched up his jeans.

"Okay, dogs, we're here to look for Billy's bird dog. Find Plato, you hear? Y'all check out the thickets and brush in the bottom of the draw and I'll ride along on the east side. Take care of your business and don't run off."

So it was true. We had been brought here to look for the Birdly Wonder. What a waste. I couldn't believe we were doing this. And something else I couldn't believe was that Beulah continued to have some odd affection for the dummy. I mean, no cow-dog in history had ever lost his way home, and no bird dog in history had ever composed poems as good . . .

Oh well. My job paid the same, whether we were doing meaningful work or searching for lost bird dogs.

I shoved these thoughts to the back of my mind, put my nose to the ground, and switched all circuits over to Smelloradar. Right away I began picking up the smells of . . . well, not much, actually. Cows, skunkbrush, wild plum leaves, aromantic sage-brush, and . . . ACHOO! . . . ragweed, but not even a whiff of anything resembling a bird dog scent.

Oh, and no coyote scent either, which was sure fine with me. I mean, with Slim riding nearby, I didn't have to worry too much about being jumped by coyotes, but still, a guy doesn't want to . . .

Huh? Singing?

I went to Full Air Brakes and lifted my ears and began scanning the horizon for sounds. Okay, it appeared to be coming from Slim, who was riding through some sagebrush hills on the other side of the draw. He was singing, if you can believe that, something like this.

Hunting for Bird Dogs

Oh the cowboy's life is wild and free,
Adventure is always at hand.
If we ain't hauling hay or milking a cow,
We're digging postholes in the sand.

> There's welding to do and garbage
>   to haul
> And painting a barn in the sun.
> But for puredee excitement, it's hard
>   to compete
> With huntin' for bird dogs on
>   November one.

I've got me a couple of pardners for this,
They're loyal and try to be strong.
The trouble is that, when the brains were
    passed out,
Old Hankie and Drover were gone.

> They're dumb but they like me, we're
>   pretty good pals,
> We have ourselves barrels of fun.

Now quail season's opened and what
    shall we do?
We're huntin' for bird dogs on
    November one.

When he'd finished his . . . whatever it was, song, I suppose . . . when he'd finished singing his pitiful little song, he looked at us and grinned. "Now, ain't that about the finest song y'all dogs have ever heard?"

I stared at him in disbelief. Was he trying to be funny? That was about the *dumbest* song I'd ever heard, certainly the dumbest I'd heard since his last dumb song. He seemed to think he was a great composer or something, and also a great singer. Ha. He didn't know beans about either one, but that didn't keep him from coming up with corny songs.

He had his nerve, suggesting that we dogs were "gone" the day the "brains were passed out." I had never been so insulted. Oh, and if he was so smart, how come we were out hunting for the neighbor's skinny stick-tailed bird dog instead of doing something constructive? If they'd asked my opinion . . .

Oh well. I can't allow myself to get worked up over all the injustice in the world. I'll say no more about it.

Yes I will. Some people seem to think that we

dogs have an easy life—chew bones, sleep all day, bark at a few cars. Well, nothing could be further from the truth. Don't forget that we're forced to listen to our masters sing songs that are insulting and corny.

Wait a minute, hold everything. *Corny. Corn. Hominy.* Was this some kind of hidden clue that might propel the case in an entirely new direction? I shot a glance at Drover, to see if he had picked it up. No, of course he hadn't, for the simple reason that he wasn't in the privy of my thought processes and therefore . . .

And therefore, just skip it.

Where were we? Oh yes, on a pointless mission to find a bird dog I didn't want to find, to save an old enemy I didn't want to save, and to waste valuable time I didn't want to waste. But there we were, and we had been ordered to . . .

All at once I was picking up new signals on Smelloradar. I lowered my sensing devicers and punched in the commands for Deep Sniff.

Sniff, sniff.

Yes, this was something new and it promised to blow the case wide open. And you know what? It did.

CHAPTER NINE

Drover Is
Cut in Half

Even though I had gotten a clear reading on Smelloradar, I decided to get a second opinion. "Drover, come here at once and tell me what this is."

He had been skipping along, looking at the clouds. He skipped over to where I was waiting. "Oh, hi. What did you say?"

I pointed to the spot where I had caught the scent. "I said, tell me what this is."

He squinted down at the ground. "Well, it looks like . . . dirt."

"Smell it, Drover, and hurry. This could be very important."

He sniffed it. "Well, it smells like . . . dirt. It looks like dirt and it smells like dirt, so I guess it's dirt."

The air hissed out of my lungs. "Please try to be

serious. There's an odd scent down there, and I want you to tell me what it might be."

He sniffed it again. "Well, let's see here. Cow manure?"

"No."

"Hominy?"

"Drover!"

He sniffed it again. This time, his eyes sprang open. "Oh my gosh, there it is. Do you reckon it's what I think it is?"

"That depends. What do you think it is?"

"Well . . . what do you think it is?"

"I thought it might be a jackrabbit."

He sniffed the spot again. "Yep, me too. It's a jackrabbit, sure 'nuff."

"Well, there we are. Two independent snifferations show positive for jackrabbit."

He beamed his patented silly grin. "Oh good, I'm so glad. I was afraid it might be a barrel hog."

"Feral hog, Drover, and no, this is nothing close to a hog scent. Hogs smell hoggy, you know."

"Yeah, it did smell kind of hoggy."

"No, I say it *didn't* smell hoggy."

He sniffed the spot again. This time, his grin faded. "Yeah, but it does. I can smell it now, and it's hoggy."

This report sent a chill down my backbone. "Did

you say hoggy or doggy? The scents are very similar, you see, and if it's a doggy smell, it might be . . . well, Plato hiding in that bush, and we'd rather find Plato than a wild hog, right? Smell it again." He did. "I'll bet it's a doggy scent, what do you say?"

When his head came up, I could see fear in his eyes. "Who's going into the bush to check it out?"

"Well, I . . . Drover, I had thought this might be a great opportunity for you to, well, take some responsibility and prove your stuff. What do you say?"

"Forget that."

"What?"

"I said . . . gosh, I'd love to, but all at once this old leg . . ."

I heaved a sigh. "Never mind, forget it, sorry I mentioned it. I'll go in myself. You'll be sorry, of course, and don't blame me when—" All at once a wild musky smell entered my nostrils. My ears jumped and a strip of hair along my backbone stood straight up. "On second thought, Drover, maybe we should, uh, bark the alarm and let Slim do the honors. We mustn't hog all the glory, so to speak."

And with that, we backed up several steps . . . quit a few steps, actually, and began lobbing Mortar Barks into the thicket. Have we discussed

Mortar Barks? It's one of the many techniques we have for blasting an enemy, and it's one of the most difficult. You have to aim high, don't you see, so that your bark arches high in the air and then falls right into the middle of the target. When it's done right, the sonic waves from the ferocious barking will come crashing down on the target and actually disable the enemy, knocking him senseless to the ground.

No kidding.

So there we were, the elite troops of the Security Division, firing off round after round of Mortar Barks and dropping them right into the middle of the plum thicket. Slim heard the roar of the barrage and came riding over to us.

"What's the deal? Y'all find something in that thicket?" He stood up in the stirrups and squinted toward the brush. "Well, I don't see anything. Come on, Snips, let's check it out."

He nudged Snips with his spurs, but Snips didn't move. He lowered his head, snorted, and backed up a step. Slim spurred him again, but the cowardly horse refused to go forward.

(See? What did I tell you? These horses prance around and talk all kinds of trash, but when it comes to action, they just can't cut the ketchup.)

(The mustard. They can't cut the mustard.)

Slim was losing his patience. "Hank, reckon you could do something that would make this crowbait move?"

Heh heh. Sure. No question about it. Not only could I do something, but I would enjoy doing it. Have we mentioned my Position on Horses? I don't like 'em, never have.

I slipped up behind the crowbait, the big cowardly crowbait, and took aim at his big fat bohunkus. *Flood tubes one and four, and plot a solution. We have a solution light! Ready, aim, FIRE!*"

Heh heh. We call this Helping Horsie Move, and fellers, he moved. Once he felt the grisp of my teeth digging into his haunch, he went airborne and flew right into the middle of the plum thicket. Old Slim lost his left stirrup and had to claw leather and hang on to the saddle horn to stay aboard.

And sure enough, something came flying out of the thicket. Maybe you think it was a jackrabbit, or stray badger, or even the Birdly Wonder himself. Nope. Remember that discussion Drover and I had held about whether the scent was "hoggy" or "doggy"? And remember that I had argued and insisted that it was "hoggy"?

Well, it was, and guess what came out. Six squealing, screaming little hoglets ... piglets ... piggies ... six baby pigs, shall we say, and they scattered in all directions. That was the good part. The bad part followed a moment later when . . . YIPES! . . . when a huge three-hundred-pound mother hog came crashing out of the thicket, and fellers, she looked mad enough to eat somebody and mean enough to do it.

Yes, it was every dog's worse nightmare, a huge inflamed wild hog momma. She glared up at Slim and Snips with flaming piggish eyes, grunted, and snapped her jaws, which were armed with long sharp tushes. Tusks. Tuskes. Teeth, big teeth.

For a moment of heartbeats, she and Slim stared into each other's eyeballs, and Slim had just enough time to say, "Boys, I think we have worn out our welcome."

He had that right. Momma Hog came flying out of the thicket, uttering horrible murderous squeals, and took aim at Snips.

Did I say that Snips was fat and lazy? Well, he might have been fat and lazy, but he sure didn't *move* fat and lazy. In the blink of an eye, he swapped ends and crashed his way out of the plum thicket. Once out of the brush, he dropped his head between his front legs and went bucking across the pasture, with Momma Hog right on his heels.

As they crested the top of a sandhill to the east, I got my last glimpse of poor Slim. He'd lost one rein and both stirrups, was sprawled across the saddle like a sack of potatoes, and was hanging on to Snips's neck for dear life, looking back with moon eyes, and yelling, "Hyah! Hyah!" at Momma Hog.

Whew! Boy, we had sure dodged a bullet there. I mean, I felt terrible that Slim had . . . well, been foolish enough to ride into that thicket, I mean, he should have waited and let us dogs go in first to, uh, test the situation, but no, he'd been in a hurry and . . . we'd tried to warn him that the thicket might contain something large and dangerous, right? I had done my best to . . .

I glanced around for Drover. At first I saw no sign of him, but then my keen eyes picked up a flash of white on the other side of the thicket. I moved around to get a better look and saw . . . hmmm . . . the hiney and stub tail of a dog sticking up, only the front half of his body was . . . missing.

Holy smokes, had the wild hog taken a slash at little Drover and cut him in half? That certainly appeared to be the case. I rushed over to the spot, expecting to see a ghastly scene, with hair and gore and puddles of blood.

"Drover, don't move, you've been cut in half! Lie still and don't try to talk. Where's your head?"

I heard his faint reply. "I'm not sure. Everything's dark."

"You're losing consciousness. Fight it, Drover, try to stay awake. I've got to find your head. Do you have any idea where it went?"

"Well . . ."

"Just lie still and don't talk. If I can find your head, maybe we can stick you back together and save you."

"I think my head's here with me."

"Oh, good. For a minute there I was afraid it had rolled off somewhere. Don't give up hope, son. Modern medicine performs miracles every day."

"Help! The darkness is closing in!"

"Fight it, Drover. Don't give up. Can you give me some hints? If your head is there with you, just tell me where you are."

"Well, let's see. I think I'm in a hole."

HUH?

It was then that I noticed . . . did you think that Drover had been cut in half? Ha, ha. No, if he'd been cut in half, we wouldn't have been carrying on a conversation, see, because . . .

He'd dug the top half of his body into a sand hole, is what he'd done, and to a casual observer it might have appeared that . . . well . . . the lower half of his body was just . . . standing there. Without a head. Or shoulders or front legs.

I marched over to him and gave him a kick in

the behind. "You can come out now, Drover. I've solved the Mystery of the Severed Head."

He pulled himself out and shook the sand off his carcass. "Oh, hi. Gosh, there for a minute, I thought . . ."

"You thought you'd been decaffeinated, but you ignored one tiny detail. At the first sign of danger, you burrowed the top half of your body into the sand. In cowardly fashion, you fled from Reality."

"Yeah, and boy, she sure looked mean. I guess she was a wild hog."

"Well, she thought she was wild . . . until I got done with her."

Drover's eyes widened. "You mean . . . you whipped her?"

"Oh, sure. She was nothing but an ugly pig, Drover, and I told her so."

"No fooling?"

"Yes, and then I gave her the thrashing she so richly deserved. I guess you heard all that squealing? She learned a bitter lesson and I don't think we'll be seeing anymore of her." It was then that I noticed the piglets. They had come together, put their heads to the center, and piled on top of each other. "Well, look at this, Drover. A pile of little piggies. Let's have a look."

I marched over to them, but Drover didn't move.

"You know, that might not be such a great idea. I mean, if . . ."

"Oh, rubbish. That old hag of a hog wouldn't dare . . ."

HUH?

CHAPTER TEN

Oh No! The Killer Hog Appears!

She'd come back.

I looked into her face and almost fainted. Her tiny piggish eyes glistened with an unhealthy light and she was snapping those powerful jaws open and shut. I swallowed hard and moved my gaze over the rest of her body. She was BIG—tall and wide, built like an iron safe and covered with stiff bristles of hair.

On instinct, I looked for a weakness I might be able to exploit if . . . well, if things got out of hand, shall we say. All animals have a weak spot, right? That's the way it's supposed to work, but you show me the weakness in a three-hundred-pound hog.

They don't have one. Their bodies are thick, their hair is thick, their skin is thick, their skulls are thick. You bite them and they don't feel it. You hit them and they don't even notice. You claw them and it doesn't even scratch the skin.

Gulp.

Clearly this was the wrong time to seek a, uh, military solution to our problem. Perhaps charm and diplomacy would work.

I beamed up my most sincere smile of friendliness and sincerity. "Why, Mrs. Hog, what a pleasant surprise! We thought . . . that is, Drover and I thought . . . that's Drover over there, my assistant . . . uh . . . Drover, meet Mrs. Hog . . . we thought you had left your piggies . . . kids . . . children . . . not that you had abandoned them, no no, only that you had, well, left them for a while, don't you see, and we were just . . ."

She stared at me and uttered a noise: "Rrrrunt, rrrrrunt."

My mouth was very dry. I licked my lips and smiled and gestured toward the stack of hoggies, the ugliest collection of creatures I had ever laid eyes on.

"They're . . . uh . . . awfully cute. Very cute. Darling."

"Rrrrrunt, rrrrunt."

"Okay, no doubt you're wondering what we're doing here, two dogs alone with your . . ." I shot a glance at the pile of piggies. Several of them had lifted their heads and were looking at me. Gag! How could anyone love something that ugly? ". . . alone with these darling little piglets. I think I can explain everything, honest."

I eased a paw over to the pile and patted one of them on the back. He squealed and bit me. "Youch! My goodness, ha ha, he's a feisty little guy, isn't he? Ha, ha. Anyway, we saw you leave a while ago,

chasing the, uh, horse and so forth, and we said to ourselves, we said, 'By George, we'd better rush over there and guard her children from the . . .'"

I glanced around, hoping to find something that would keep my story moving, you know, something that might draw her attention away from me. Nothing. But then my gaze drifted up to the sky, and there I saw . . . aha! Yes, two big black birds wheeling above us, and they even appeared to be coming in for a landing.

Perfect!

I licked my dry lips and continued. "And so I said to Drover, 'Drover, by George, we had better get over there and protect Mrs. Hog's children from an attack by those *two huge hungry eagles.*'"

I pointed to the sky. Her gaze followed my point.

"Rrrunt, rrrunt."

I plunged on. "As you surely know, ma'am, your eagles and your hawks and your owls are very fond of . . . well, pork chops, shall we say."

"Rrrrrrrunt?"

"Oh yes, they dearly love your various cuts of pork, whereas we dogs . . . ha, ha, well, we wouldn't even think of harming a little . . . " I patted another of the homely little things on the . . . good grief, he bit me too! "Avast, you little Martian!" I turned a quick smile on Momma. "I mean, heh heh, they're shy around strangers, aren't they? But cute, very cute."

I swallowed the cotton in my throat and mushed on. "Anyway, we perceived that there was some threat, a huge threat, to your . . . " I pointed to the buzzards, who were gliding in for a landing. "There, you see? Here they come, even as we speak. Eagles."

As you might have guessed, it was Wallace and Junior, the buzzards, and they couldn't have come at a better time. Even at a distance, I could see the crazed smile on Wallace's face, and could hear him yelling.

"Flaps down, son! Bring 'er down easy and watch out for trees!" He glided in, clipped a sagebrush, did two flips in the air, hit the ground with a thud, and rolled to a stop. He didn't miss a beat, but leaped to his feet and came hopping over to us. Behind him, Junior crashed beak-first into the sand.

Momma Hog grunted and took a step backward.

Here came the old man. "Well, I see we ain't too late for a nice doggie dinner, and yes, this is indeed a happy day in our lives, and Junior, I get first dibs on the drumsticks." He grinned a wild grin and rubbed his wings together. "Hello, dog, looks like y'all have fell on hard times, but we sure appreciate the business, we truly do. Me and Junior ain't had but three scraps of dead snake in two weeks, and, son, you'd best get yourself over here, I ain't sure I can hold myself back."

Junior came waddling up, huffing and puffing and spitting sand. "H-h-here I c-c-come, P-pa, and oh m-m-my g-g-g-goodness, it's our d-d-d-doggie friend." He gave me a shy grin and waved his wing. "H-h-hi there, d-d-d-doggie."

I dipped my head in greeting. "How's it going, Junior?"

"Oh w-w-well, b-b-busy, b-b-busy."

Wallace stuck his beak into my face. "I'll tell you how it's going, puppy dog. Times is hard. Our business is off thirty percent. Last month, road kill was down forty-two percent. We're just a-struggling to make ends meet, is how hard our life is."

"W-w-well P-pa, w-we d-did f-f-find that uh uh d-d-dead skunk t-t-two days ago, days ago."

Wallace gave him a glare. "I ain't a-counting that skunk, Junior. It had been smushed by a big old truck and there wasn't nothing left but hair and grease, and you ate the grease."

"W-w-w-well, I g-g-got there f-f-first."

"You got there first because you cheated, is how you done it." Wallace turned to me. "He cheated. My own son, my own flesh and blood cheated me out of a dandy little puddle of skunk grease."

"N-n-n-no, I g-g-got there f-f-first because y-y-

100

you s-stepped in a h-h-h-hole and f-f-fell down, fell down."

"I did not step in a hole, I have never stepped in a hole, you cheated your poor old daddy, I seen it with my very own eyes, and son, I haven't yet got over the shock and dismay of . . ." He whirled back to me. "I'm running on skunk hair, is how bad times are, but I can see that business is fixing to pick up." He jerked his head around to Momma Hog. "Well? What are you waiting for? Let's get this thang started. We'll settle for a fifty percent chunk of the deal."

"Rrrrrunt, rrrrunt!"

"Okay, sixty-forty." He turned back to me with wide eyes. "You know, that may be the ugliest woman I ever laid eyes on. You see them teeth? If I had such long old crooked teeth, I'd . . . what is she, some kind of go-rilla?"

"She's a wild hog."

"Huh. Well, she's sure filled up with the ugly, ain't she? If I was that ugly . . ." All at once a grin flashed across his beak. "Say there, neighbor, did you say she was a hog? Do you mean like a pig? Pork?" His eyes glittered and moved over to the pile of piggies. "Glory be, what do we have here?"

"P-p-pa, y-y-you'd b-b-better w-w-watch what you s-s-say, watch what you say."

"Hush, son, I'm just a-thinking out loud, and the last time I checked, there wasn't no laws against thinking." He waddled over to the piggies. Momma Hog watched and bristled. "Why, ain't they the cutest little thangs you ever saw? How precious! And just the right size for a sandwich."

"P-p-p-pa, I think y-y-y-you'd b-b-better . . ."

"You know, Junior, we come here with dog on our minds, but it never hurts to shop around." He leaned over and gave the piggies a big buzzardly smile. "Hi. How y'all? Son, the trouble with dog meat is it's awful tough and stringy."

"P-p-pa, d-d-don't g-g-get g-g-g-greedy."

"I ain't greedy, I've never been greedy, it ain't my nature. All I'm saying is . . ." He licked his chops and gave Junior a wink. "Son, I have never met a pig that could count past five, and there's six little piggies in this pile. Do you reckon she'd miss just one?"

Junior rolled his eyes. "P-p-pa, d-d-don't d-do this. Y-y-you're f-f-fixing to . . ."

"I'm just a-talking out loud, son, and there's no harm in that." He licked his beak and shot a cunning glance over to Momma Hog. "Now if I was to pick up one of these little fellers and kindly wander around behind this plum thicket, and if you was to meet me over there behind the thicket, I've got a hunch that . . ."

"P-p-pa, p-p-please."

"Son, she's got more children than she can take care of. Why, you might even say that we'd be doing her a favor." All at once he turned to me. "What do you think, dog? We could always save you for another day."

"It'll work, Wallace, great idea. She'd never miss one. I mean, she just a pig, right? And it's common knowledge that pigs can't count past five."

He draped his wing over my shoulder. "Dog, all these years I have read you wrong, I've thought you was just a dumb dog, but all at once, you're speaking truth and wisdom. Did you hear what he said, Junior? Our luck is fixing to change."

Junior gave his head a sad shake. "Y-y-yeah, it's f-f-fixing to ch-change, all r-r-r-right, and I've g-g-g-g-g-got a p-p-p-pretty g-g-g-g-good idea . . ."

Wallace scowled. "Just spit it out, son, time's a-wasting. Speak your mind, but hurry."

"I've g-g-got an idea wh-wh-wh . . . oh, j-just s-s-s-skip it, skip it."

Wallace shrugged and looked at me. "He's always been slow, that boy has. Got it from his momma. All the birds on that side of the tree was . . ." He tapped himself on the head. Then a sly grin slithered across his beak. "Oh my goodness, is that a giraffe walking over yonder? Lookie there!"

All eyes turned to the east—even the eyes of Momma Hog. See, this was part of Wallace's plan for getting a pork sandwich. When Momma Hog's eyes moved away, Wallace sprang into action. He grabbed up one of the little piggies in his clawed foot and started hopping away on one leg.

"Here we go, son! Meet you on the other side of the bushes, and hurry, first chance you get!"

At that point, things started happening fast. The little piggy let out the most incredible blurd-cuddling squeal you can imagine, and that DID get Momma's attention. Her head shot around and her eyes focused on the hopping buzzard.

"Rrrrrunt, rrrrrunt!"

Maybe you thought pigs were slow, just because they're big. Ha. In the blink of an eye, that angry mother went from a dead stop to a dead run, and she was on top of Wallace before he even knew she was coming. WHAM! Feathers flew in all directions, and so did Old Man Wallace.

"Hyah, pig, hyah! Junior, get yourself over here and help your poor old . . . son, this woman has lost her mind and you're fixing to lose your pa if you don't . . . hyah, pig, sooey!"

Junior shook his head and started taxiing into the wind. "I t-t-tried to t-t-tell you, P-p-pa, b-b-but y-y-you w-w-w-wouldn't l-listen, wouldn't listen. G-g-good l-l-luck."

"Good luck, my foot! Junior, you get yourself . . ."

Suddenly I saw our opportunity to make a run for it. I rushed over to—can you guess what Drover had been doing through all this? He had gone back to the hole in the sand and had stuck his head in it. I whopped him on the bohunkus and yelled, "Come on, Drover! Hit Full Flames and let's get out of here!"

CHAPTER ELEVEN

The Giant Snout-Nosed Quail

His head came out of the sand. His eyes were as big as pies and his teeth were chattering. "Is it safe?"

"I can't guarantee that it's safe to do anything, son, but we need to get out of here, real fast, before that mother hog decides to come after us."

"Oh my gosh! What about my bad leg?"

"Bring it. I have a feeling you'll need it before we get out of this deal!"

And with that, we went to Full Flames on all engines, and went roaring up the sand draw, crashing through sagebrush and plum thickets and bending huge trees in the wake of our jet engines. Boy, you should have seen us. No dogs in recent history had ever made such an amazing escape from danger.

Oh, and you might be interested to know that Drover ran just as fastly as I did. There was no trace of a limp on his so-called bad leg. Are you shocked? Not me. See, sometimes I think that leg of his is just . . . oh well, we made our escape, that was the important thing.

We must have run, oh, half a mile, before we dared to stop and catch our breath. "Nice work, son, but that was a little too close for comfort."

The little mutt rolled his eyes around. "Yeah, but don't you think we should have run south instead of north? Now we're farther away from Billy's house than ever."

I ran my gaze around the immediate vicinity. Hmmm. He had a point. "Drover, every once in a while you come up with a good idea. I just wish you would speak up sooner."

"Well . . ."

"Never mind. It won't matter. We'll find our way back in due time. The important thing is that we've escaped the wild hog."

"You don't think she'll follow our scent?"

"Scent? Drover, it's common knowledge that hogs can't follow a scent. Do you know why? Hogs smell so bad, they can't smell."

"Yeah, and they can't count past five either."

"What? I wish you wouldn't mutter."

Rrrrunt, rrrrunt!

"What? There you go again. If you have some-thing to say, step up to the plate and pick up the fork and speak your mind."

"Yeah, but . . . that wasn't me."

"Of course it was you. Who else . . ."

Rrrrrunt! Rrrrrunt! Rrrrrunt!

My eyes popped wide open. I swallowed a lump in my throat. "Did you hear that?"

"Yeah, I heard it."

"And it wasn't you? Are you sure? Hey listen, if it was you, just say so and forget what I said about muttering."

"It wasn't me. And you know what I think?"

"You think that maybe pigs have a better sense of smell than you thought, right? I'm beginning to have that same feeling, Drover, and furthermore . . ."

Rrrrunt! Rrrrrunt! Rrrrrunt!

The sound was coming from a spot down the sand draw, and it was getting closer. Gulp.

"Drover, the pieces of the puzzle are falling to pieces. We need to move our camp and get the heck out of here, because you see, the sounds we are hear-ing might very well be coming from . . ."

ZOOM! He was already gone, streaking north up the draw. I had to run hard to catch up with him.

"Drover, I didn't give the command to leave,

and I notice that your leg is doing much better."

"Yeah, even a blind hog can cure a limp."

"What? Come back on that, son, it didn't make much . . ."

HUH?

You won't believe this. I could hardly believe it myself. It was a stroke of incredibly bad luck. See, at the very moment when it appeared that we had made our escape from the crazed mother hog, I looked up ahead and saw—oh no!

It was the Coyote Brotherhood, Rip and Snort the cannibal brothers, sitting out in the middle of the sand draw. Pretty scary, huh? You bet it was. I mean, if a guy was alone in a big pasture, miles away from the nearest outpost of civilization, the last thing he'd want to see . . .

We came to a screeching halt and managed to get things shut down. The brothers hadn't seen or heard us, which was good. What wasn't so good was that somewhere down the sand draw, a relentless, indestructible wild hog was following our scent. Within minutes, she would find us.

Gulp. I turned to my assistant. "Drover, I don't want to alarm you, but our situation seems to be getting worse by the minute."

"Yeah, I was afraid of that. I want to go home!"

"Great idea, Drover. Why don't you do that?

Head for the house and maybe that wild hog will help you find the way."

"Help, murder, Mayday! Oh my leg!"

He was worthless. I tore my attention away from Mister Moan and Groan and peered through some bushes that stood between us and the coyote brothers. It was then that I noticed . . .

"Holy smokes, Drover, do you see what I see?"

"No! All at once everything's dark. I think I fainted. Help!"

I glanced back at him and saw that he was lying on the ground with his paws over his eyes. "Get up, Drover, and pay attention. Do you see who's with the coyotes? It's Plato, and unless I'm badly mistaken, he's teaching them how to hunt quail."

Rrrrunt! Rrrunt!

My ears flew up. Mother Hog was getting closer.

"Drover, if you had a choice between being torn to shreds by a herd of wild hogs or being eaten by cannibals, which would you choose?"

"Is there a third choice?"

"I'm afraid not. No, it appears . . . wait a minute, hold everything. Why shouldn't there be a third choice? Why should we be limited to two choices, both equally bad? Recent studies show that there are a hundred and forty-seven choices in this world, so yes, Drover, let's choose Number Three!"

There was a moment of silence. "Okay, but what is it?"

"Well, I was hoping you might have something in mind. Something. Anything. Hurry, Drover, I hate to rush you, but those hogs . . ." I could see them now, coming up the draw with their snouts to the ground. "Okay, Drover, we're about to take some drastic action. I don't know what it'll be, but stick with me and follow my lead."

I took a big gulp of air, rose to an upright position, smeared a calm smile across my mouth, and marched right into the middle of the Coyote Brotherhood. Rip and Snort were sitting near a wild plum bush, staring with expressionless yellow eyes at Plato, who was demonstrating the proper techniques for hunting quail.

"Okay, fellas," said Plato, "the next thing on the list is the Sniffing Position. Very important, very important. I can't emphasize that enough. Technique is everything. Here, watch this." He went into this hunting stance. "You see? Throw that tail out, stiff and straight. Stretch out the body like this, and then drop the nose to a point just inches above the ground. Try it, fellas."

The brothers grumbled and exchanged whispers, but then pushed themselves up and went into their Sniffing Positions. Plato watched them, shaking his head and rolling his eyes.

"Okay, fellas, that's not bad for a first try, but we've got some room for improvement." He walked over to Snort. "Bend those front legs . . . what was your name again?"

"Name Snort."

"Great. You've got to bend those front legs, Snork. Crouch. Get into position. That's better, and stiffen that tail. It needs to be as straight as a stick."

"Snort not have stick tail like bird dog. Got fluffy tail."

"Right, I understand, Snork. We all have our own unique gifts, but the tail must be stiff. And get that nose down closer to the ground."

Plato pushed Snort's nose down and drove it into the sand. Snort's head shot up and his eyes

were burning. "Bird dog not shove Snort nose into stupid sand!"

Plato heaved a sigh. "Sorry, but listen, fellas, you wanted the quick course on birding and we've got a lot of material to cover in a very short time. I'm on a tight schedule here and I need to get back to the ranch."

Rip and Snort exchanged grins. "Ha, ha. Bird dog got plenty time. Not need to get in big hurry-up."

Plato's smile began to wilt. "Now fellas . . . we talked about this and I made it perfectly clear that I had to . . . you're laughing. Did I say something funny? Fellas?"

The brothers stood up and turned menacing eyes on Plato. "Fellas not give a hoot for perfectly clear. Fellas not give a hoot for bird-finder stuff. Fellas thinking about . . . eat teacher, ho ho."

Plato's eyes bugged out. "Now wait just a darn . . . that was *not* in the bargain we made. We agreed . . . I remember this very . . . you said . . ." He took a step backward. "Fellas, eating me was NOT part of our arrangement, and let me be very candid here. If I had known . . ."

His words were drowned out by their laughter. "Ha, ha! Bird dog pretty dumb for make deal with Rip and Snort. Bird dog pretty dumb for leave house and boom-boom. And bird dog make snack for Rip and Snort, ho ho."

"Snack? Listen, fellas, I'm sure we can . . . this wasn't . . . you can't . . . HELP!" Plato was so scared he couldn't say another word.

It was time for me to make my move, even though I still wasn't sure what it would be. I took a deep breath, put on my most confident air, and marched right into the middle of them.

"Oh, Plato, there you are. Listen, bud, I don't suppose you've seen a couple of coyotes named Rip and Snort, have you? Big guys, dashing and hand-some, very intelligent? We've got to find them right away. I've got some terrific news for 'em."

Plato stared at me with huge disbelieving eyes. Then he made a grimace, jerked his gaze toward the brothers, and croaked, "There. Help!"

I turned to the coyotes and beamed them a smile. "Oh, there you are! By George, I've been look-ing all over for you guys. Where have you been?"

Snort gave me a suspicious scowl. "Been here. Been busy learning bird-find. Been hungry and fix-ing to eat dummy bird dog, oh boy."

"Eat the bird dog? That's pretty crude, guys. I mean, the whole idea is to find quail."

"Quail-bird too little and hard to catch, always run and fly away. Bird dog easy to catch."

"Yeah, but he's too skinny. What you guys need to find is a covey of . . . of Giant Snout-Nosed Quail."

There you are, and now you know the plan I had hatched to get us out of there. Would it work? Would Rip and Snort fall for my trick? I held my breath and waited.

You'll just have to do the same. Or else you could keep reading.

CHAPTER TWELVE

Unbelievable Ending! No Kidding

I studied the coyotes to see if they would take the bait. Their faces showed . . . nothing. Zero. Not a hint of thought or emotion.

I turned to Plato. "You *did* tell 'em about the Giant Snout-Nosed Quail, didn't you?" I gave him a wink.

"Help."

"I guess not." I turned back to the brothers. "Plato forgot to tell you. Giant Snout-Nosed Quail are what you want. Don't waste your time with these little bobwhites and blues. If you're really hungry, go for the big ones."

Snort stepped up to me and stuck his sharp nose in my face. "Rip and Snort not see Big Snot-Nosed Quail-birds, only little chirp-chirps."

"Well, let me describe them. They're big, Snort, huge. They have ears, long floppy ears, and their feathers look like bristles. And they have a long . . . uh . . . beak that looks very much like a snout. Honest. No kidding."

The brothers glared at me, then shook their heads. "Brothers not believe Hunk, 'cause Hunk always telling coyote brothers big stupid whoppers. Maybe Rip and Snort eat bird dog, then eat Hunk and little white dog too, ho ho."

"What? You don't believe me? After all the years and the good times we've . . . okay, guys, you want me to tell you how to find these giant quail? I'll tell you, but you must promise never to reveal this to anyone. Promise?"

Snort clubbed me over the head with his paw. "Snort promise to break Hunk face. Hurry up."

"Okay, fine. Here's the scoop. These giant quail make an unusual sound. They don't whistle or chirp like your ordinary quail. They make a bigger, deeper sound, kind of like . . . let me see if I can make the sound. *Runt, runt.* That's it. If you ever hear that, you'll know that Giant Snout-Nosed Quail are close."

The coyotes stared at me with empty yellow eyes. "Runt runt? Ha. Rip and Snort not fall for Hunk stupid story about snot-nose runt-runt bird."

Just then . . . you won't believe this, I mean the timing was perfect . . . just then, we heard a sound coming up the sand draw. *Rrrrrunt! Rrrrrunt!* Rip's ears shot up. Snort's ears shot up. They exchanged puzzled glances.

I pushed on with this incredible fraud, hoping that somehow . . . "There! Did you hear that? Didn't I tell you? There's your proof, guys. Those huge juicy quail are coming up the draw this very minute. Oh, but there's one other thing, Snort. They're not only big, but they're tough. They don't fight like ordinary quail, so we'd better let Plato show you how to handle them. What do you say, Plato, are you ready to go?"

"Help."

"He's ready to go, so just stand back and let him . . ."

Snort swept me aside with his paw and gave me a big toothy grin. "Rip and Snort not need help from skinny bird dog, and not scared of big runt-runt birds."

"I don't know, guys, they're pretty tough."

"Ha! Rip and Snort meaner and meanest, tear up whole world in fight, not scared of nothing." They flexed their muscles and cut loose with chilling howls. Just then, Momma Hog rounded a bend in the draw. She saw them and they saw her. They all froze. Then Snort said, "Uh. That pretty big runt-runt bird, all right."

I rushed over to them. "Now Snort, if you think she's too big . . . the important thing here is to remember your lessons. Technique. Throw out that tail, crouch down low, and put your nose—"

You know what he did? He pushed my nose into the sand!

"Hunk talk too much. Coyote not give a hoot for techneep, just beat 'em up and eat, ho ho."

Rip muttered his agreement, and the two of them started slouching down the draw toward Momma Hog and her brood. When the little piggies saw what was coming their way—two big scruffy evil-looking coyotes—they squealed and took cover in the nearest bush. That left Momma Hog to face the approach of the brothers.

Rip and Snort had no idea what they were walking into, but I did, and it was time to prepare for Phase Two. I turned to Plato, who was staring off into space with glassy eyes. "Plato, get ready to run."

He was frozen by fear and croaked, "Help."

"When the fight starts, we've got to haul the mail out of here, understand?"

"Help."

I lifted the flap of his right ear and stuck my

nose into it and yelled, *"Listen, birdbrain, we've come to save you!"*

His eyes came into focus. "What? Where am I? Hank? Is that you? Listen, I just met two of the biggest, meanest stray dogs—"

"They're coyotes, Plato, and they have every intention of eating you."

He frowned at me for a moment. "Coyotes? Oh my gosh! I knew there was something strange about those two. I'm scared to death of coyotes, did you know that?"

"Can you run?"

He gave that some thought. "You know, Hank, I don't think so. I mean, the trauma of this is so great . . ."

Off to the right, we heard the first sounds of battle: first, the piercing squeal of Momma Hog, then loud crashing and banging and growling, and then . . . the squealing of two very surprised cannibals.

I looked Plato in the eyes. "We've got to get out of here, fast, and I'm not going to carry you. For some weird reason, Beulah wants to see you again."

He smiled. "Really? Bunny Cakes? You know, Hank, maybe the memory of her will propel me back to the ranch."

"Great. Let's go."

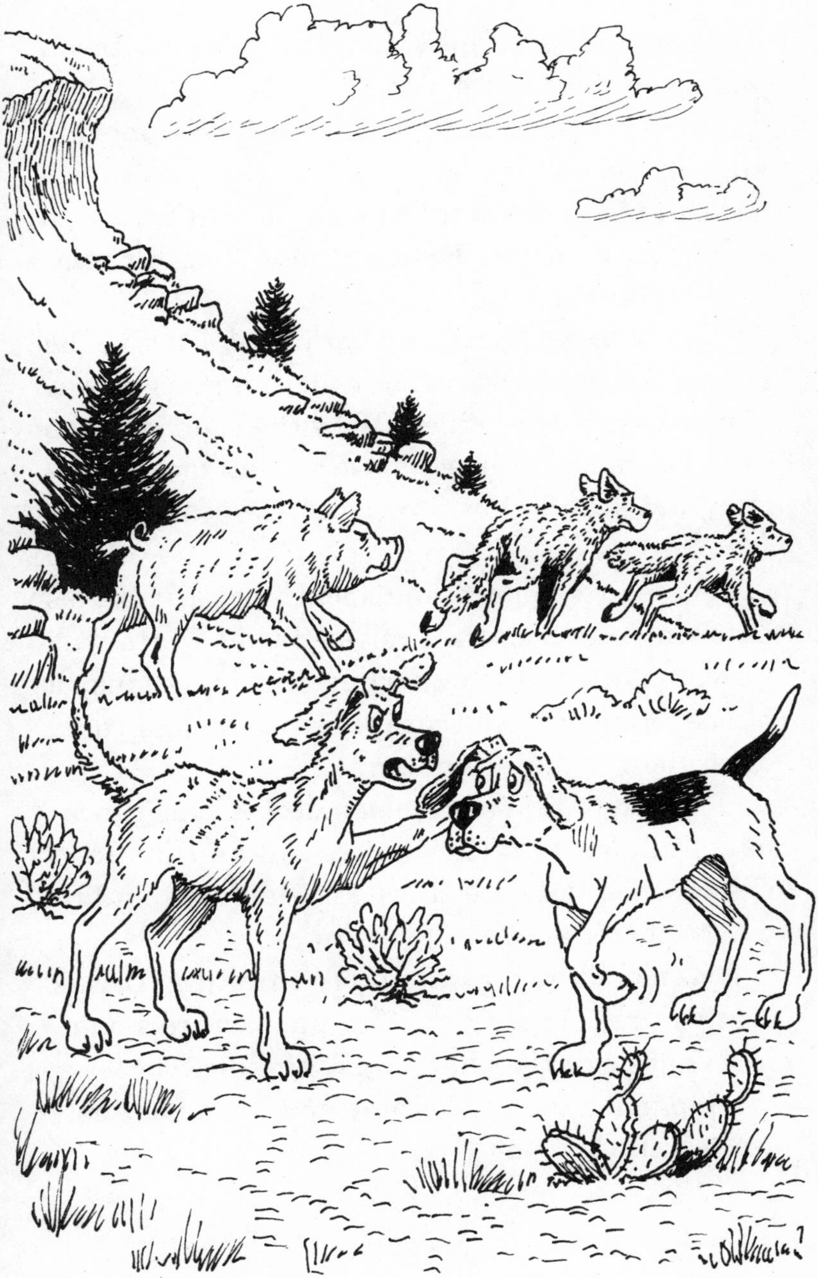

"I really appreciate this, Hank, and I mean that from the bottom of my—"

"Will you dry up? Drover, get up, we're moving out. Go, go, go!"

Can you believe it? Plato was still trying to make idle chatter! "Hank, I know that our relationship has—"

I gave him a shove and got him started in the right direction. I hated to be rude, but this guy was about to get us all killed. With the sounds of the battle echoing in our ears, we set sail for civilization and didn't slow down until we saw Billy's windmill up ahead.

There, we stopped and spent several minutes catching our breath. I noticed that Plato was watching me, and after a while he said, "Thanks a bunch, Hank. I wish there was something I could do to show my appreciation."

I stared at him for a long moment, this ridiculous buffoon with the skinny tail and the long floppy ears. "Maybe there is, Plato, old buddy, maybe there is."

"Hank, I know what you're thinking. It was pretty dumb of me to go off in the pasture alone."

"That's exactly what I was thinking."

"I bungled the whole thing and could have gotten us killed."

"Right."

"I don't know why I do such things, Hank, but I do. All I can say is . . . I'm a bird dog, and sometimes bird dogs do . . . silly things."

"So it seems."

He looked off in the distance. "You don't understand that, do you? No, you're a cowdog. You don't know how it feels to be awkward and frightened, how it feels to make stupid mistakes all the time. Well, I do. It just seems to be my fate."

"How interesting."

"But you know, Hank, the one thing that keeps me going . . . the one light that shines in my darkest hours is . . . Beulah." My eyes rolled up inside my head. He went on. "We're fond of each other, you know. I can't imagine what she sees in a blundering idiot like me, but . . . she sees something, Hank. Isn't that a miracle?" He turned to me. "By golly, Hank, I think something's wrong with your eyes. They seem to be rolled up in your head. Here, let me help you lie down."

"Get away from me, you—"

"It must be an adrenalin rush. That happens to me all the time during bird season, the excitement, I guess. Just lie down and be still. There! Oh, good, great, here comes Beulah. Beulah? Bunny Cakes? I've come back!"

They rushed into each other's embrace. I thought seriously about throwing up to celebrate the occasion, but didn't want to waste a good meal. They came skipping over to me, all smiles and sparkling eyes.

Beulah laid a paw on my shoulder. "Oh, Hank, you're so brave and heroic! Thank you for everything you've done. I only wish there was some way we could show our appreciation."

Plato stepped forward. "Bunny Cakes, I said the very same thing to old Hank, and by golly, he said there might be one thing we could do, right Hank?"

Beulah looked at me. "Really? What is it, Hank? Just tell us."

I ran my gaze over their faces—their broad smiles, their shimmering eyes. They were both so happy. And so *dumb*. I heaved a sigh and cranked myself up off the ground.

"Don't worry about it. It's all in a day's work, just part of the job."

Plato gasped. "Did you hear that, Sweetsy? What a guy! Hank, we're just speechless."

"Right."

"I'm at a total loss for words. All I can say is," he whopped me on the back, "one of these days, by golly, you'll be rewarded for all the wonderful things you do."

I stared at him and words began marching across the parade ground of my mind. *"Yes, and when I get my reward, you'll have a black eye and one less girlfriend."*

Just then, Slim and Billy came running out of the yard. For my heroic rescue of the bird dog, I received three pats on the head and two "Good dogs." Moments later, we were in Slim's pickup, heading back to the ranch. Plato and Beulah waved good-bye, and as they disappeared from view, I saw Plato place his paw on her shoulder.

I turned to Drover. "What are you staring at?"

He sniffed his nose and a tear slid down his cheek. "Well, I don't know. Everything turned out so perfect. Mother Pig saved her piggies and you saved Plato, and now Plato and Beulah are back together and you're a hero and . . . and it's such a wonderful ending, I think I'll just . . . cry!"

I gave him a minute to boo-hoo and blubber. "Drover, allow me to raise one small question."

He sniffed his nose and got control of himself. "Okay, sure. I just hope I know the answer."

"If I'm such a hero and if this is such a happy ending, how come Plato's back there with Beulah, and I'm riding in a pickup with *you*?"

He blinked his eyes. "Well, I don't know. I never thought about that."

"Well, think about it. When you come up with the answer, wake me up. I'm going to sleep. Good night, Drover."

"Good night, Hank . . . only it's still daylight."

"Hush!"

And so it was that I ended another grueling day of fighting monsters, protecting my ranch from evil forces, and rescuing homeless bird dogs, and drifted off into a fragrant dream about—mercy! Was it . . . could it be . . . ? Yes, there stood Missy Coyote in the distance, gazing at me with adoring eyes and calling my . . . snork murk snicklefritz honking porkchops . . . zzzzzzz.

Cose clazed.

Case closed, let us say.

The following activities are samples from *The Hank Times*, the official newspaper of Hank's Security Force. Do not write on these pages unless this is your book. Even then, why not just find a scrap of paper?

Rhyme Time

Rip decides to leave coyote country to get a job. What jobs could he do?

Make a rhyme using the name Rip that would relate to the jobs below.

Example: Rip could be the opposite of a bump in the road: Rip DIP

1. Rip could be a leaky faucet.

2. Rip starts a travel agency and plans this for people.

3. Rip invents a new kind of spinning high dive.

4. Rip could be something found on your face.

5. Rip could be a blinking dot on an air controller's screen.

6. Rip gives a helpful hint in his newspaper advice column.

7. Rip could be a thing to hold papers together.

8. Rip teaches manners: Don't take a big gulp. Take a small drink.

9. Rip could be the way you hold something.

10. Rip becomes a big boat.

Eye-Crosserosis

I've done it again. I was staring at the end of my nose and had my eyes crossed for a long time. And you know what? They got hung up—my eyes, I mean. I couldn't get them uncrossed. It's a serious condition called Eye-Crosserosis. (You can read about the big problems Eye-Crosserosis caused me in my second book.) This condition throws everything out of focus, as you can see. Can you help me turn the double letters and word groupings below into words?

Insert the double letters into the word groupings to form words you can find in my books.

DD	RR	OO	SS	EE	TT
PP	LL	ZZ	UU	DD	GG

1. MIOR_____

2. PUY_____

3. BIROG_____

4. MNBEAMS_____

5. VACM_____

6. SALE_____

7. BUARD_____

8. GRN_____

9. MIING_____

10. CALE_____

11. DOIE_____

12. WAACE_____

Answers:

1. MIRROR
2. PUPPY
3. BIRDDOG
4. MOONBEAMS
5. VACUUM
6. SADDLE
7. BUZZARD
8. GREEN
9. MISSING
10. CATTLE
11. DOGGIE
12. WALLACE

"Photogenic" Memory Quiz

We all know that Hank has a "photogenic" memory—being aware of your surroundings is an important quality for a Head of Ranch Security. Now you can test your powers of observation.

How good is your memory? Look at the illustration on page 47 and try to remember as many things about it as possible. Then turn back to this page and see how many questions you can answer.

1. Was Slim wearing a belt?

2. Could you see Hank's tongue, Drover's tongue, or both of their tongues?

3. Did Slim's shirt have 0, 1, or 2 pockets?

4. Was Slim's left hand or right hand on the fence post?

5. How many clouds were there—1, 2, or 3?

6. How many ears could you see on Hank, Drover, and Slim—5, 6, or 7?

Have you read all of Hank's adventures?

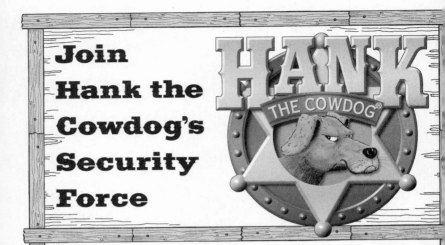

□ Yes, I want to join Hank's Security Force. Enclosed is $11.95 ($8.95 + $3.00 for shipping and handling) for my **two-year membership**. [Make check payable to Maverick Books.]

Which book would you like to receive in your Welcome Package? Choose any book in the series.

(#   )   (#   )
FIRST CHOICE   SECOND CHOICE

                                         BOY or GIRL
YOUR NAME   (CIRCLE ONE)

MAILING ADDRESS

CITY   STATE   ZIP

TELEPHONE   BIRTH DATE

E-MAIL

Are you a □ Teacher or □ Librarian?

Send check or money order for $11.95 to:

Hank's Security Force
Maverick Books
P.O. Box 549
Perryton, Texas 79070

DO NOT SEND CASH. NO CREDIT CARDS ACCEPTED.
Allow 4–6 weeks for delivery.

The Hank the Cowdog Security Force, the Welcome Package, and The Hank Times *are the sole responsibility of Maverick Books. They are not organized, sponsored, or endorsed by Penguin Putnam Inc., Puffin Books, Viking Children's Books, or their subsidiaries or affiliates.*